H.G. WELLS'S

THE WAR OF THE WORLDS

A GRAPHIC NOVEL

BY DAVIS WORTH MILLER,
KATHERINE MCLEAN BREVARD, &
JOSÉ ALFONSO OCAMPO RUIZ

STONE ARCH BOOKS
A CAPSTONE IMPRINT

Graphic Revolve is published by Stone Arch Books
A Capstone Imprint
1710 Roe Crest Drive, North Mankato, Minnesota 56003
www.capstonepub.com

Cataloging-in-Publication Data is available at the Library
of Congress website.
Hardcover ISBN: 978-1-4965-0018-2
Paperback ISBN: 978-1-4965-0037-3

Summary: In the late 19th century, a cylinder crashes
down near London. When George investigates, a
Martian activates an evil machine and begins destroying
everything in its path! George must find a way to survive
a War of the Worlds

Common Core back matter written by Dr. Katie Monnin.

Color by Jorge Gonzalez/Protobunker Studio.

Designer: Bob Lentz
Assistant Designer: Peggie Carley
Editor: Donald Lemke
Assistant Editor: Sean Tulien
Creative Director: Heather Kindseth
Editorial Director: Michael Dahl
Publisher: Ashley C. Andersen Zantop

Printed in the United States of America in
North Mankato, Minnesota.
092018   000046

TABLE OF CONTENTS

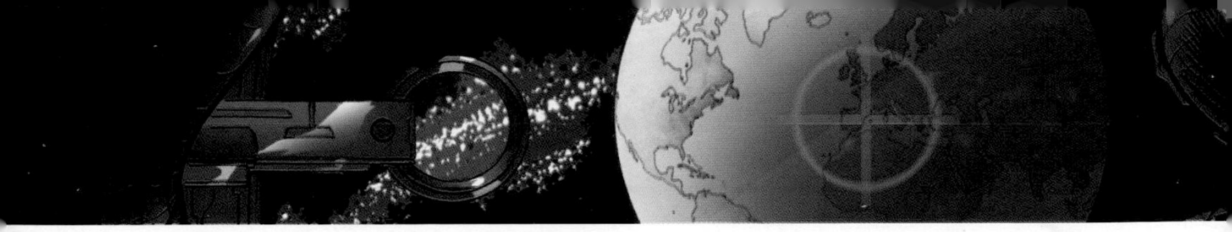

"THE WAR OF THE WORLDS" ON THE RADIO

On October 30, 1938, an announcer for CBS Radio started his broadcast with a warning: he told his listeners that for the next 60 minutes they'd be hearing a play based on the H.G. Wells novel, *The War of the Worlds*. Unfortunately, many people tuned in late and never heard the introduction.

As the show started, the radio's music was quickly interrupted by a breaking news bulletin. It said a "huge flaming object" had struck a farm near Grover's Mill, New Jersey. A reporter on the scene described seeing an alien crawl out of a spacecraft. "Good heavens, something's wriggling out of the shadow," he said. "I can see the thing's body now. It's large — large as a bear. It glistens like wet leather."

Later reports detailed that Newark, New Jersey, had been destroyed by Martian invaders. The reports stated that the aliens were on their way to New York City, which was being evacuated. Other invaders had been spotted near Washington, Buffalo, Chicago, and other cities around the country.

Of course, all of these "reports" of aliens were just part of the radio show. Still, thousands of people believed the attacks were real. They called newspapers, radio stations, and police headquarters, asking how to protect themselves from the aliens.

Hundreds of people needed medical treatment for shock. Terrified listeners hid in their cellars and loaded their rifles. In the area around New York City, highways became jammed with cars. Train and bus stations were choked with terrified people trying to leave the city.

In all, about one million people believed that they were listening to a real alien invasion. As the show ended, those people soon realized that they had been tricked. The entire show was simply a Halloween gag performed by 23-year-old Orson Welles and a group of actors.

Welles would later become one of the most famous movie directors in Hollywood.

CAST OF CHARACTERS

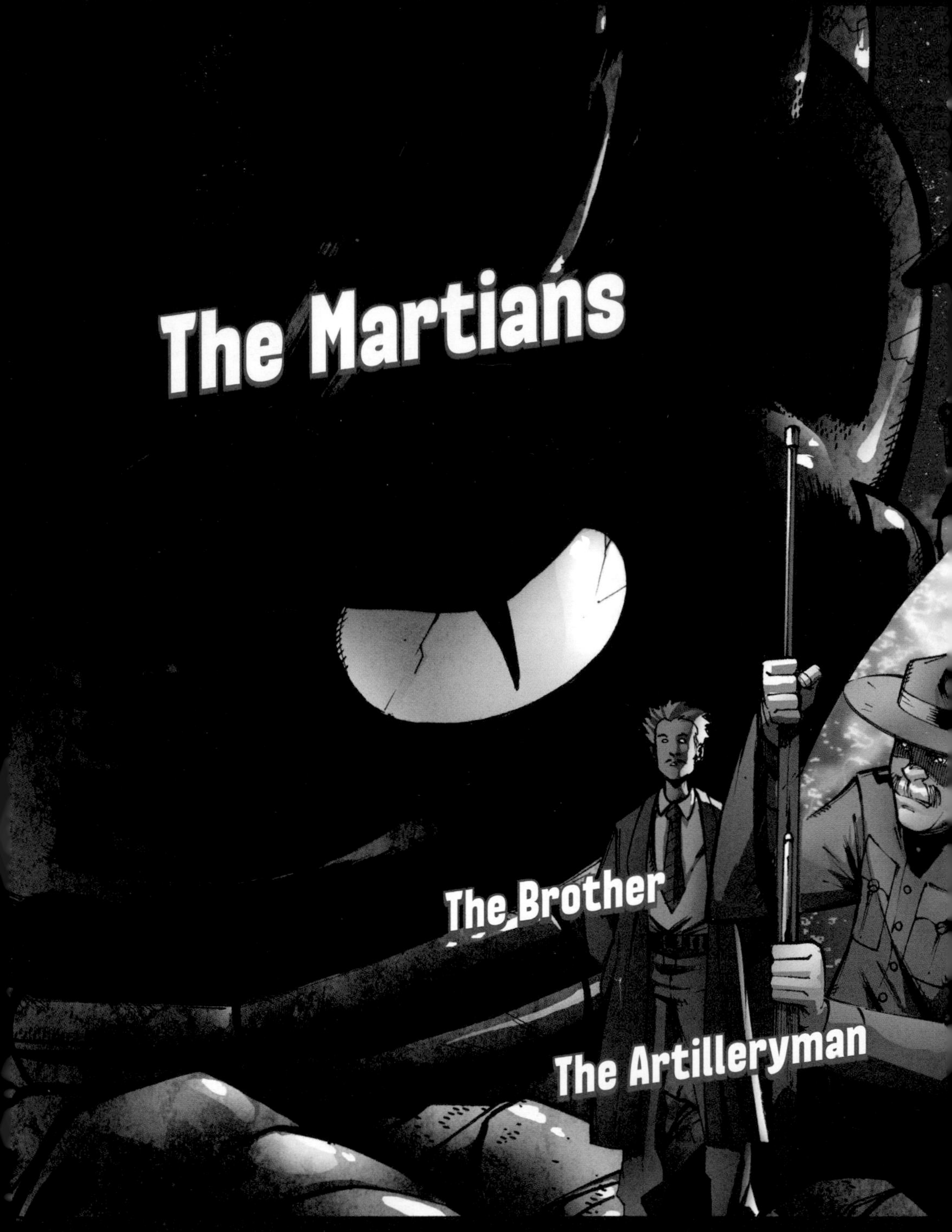
The Martians
The Brother
The Artilleryman

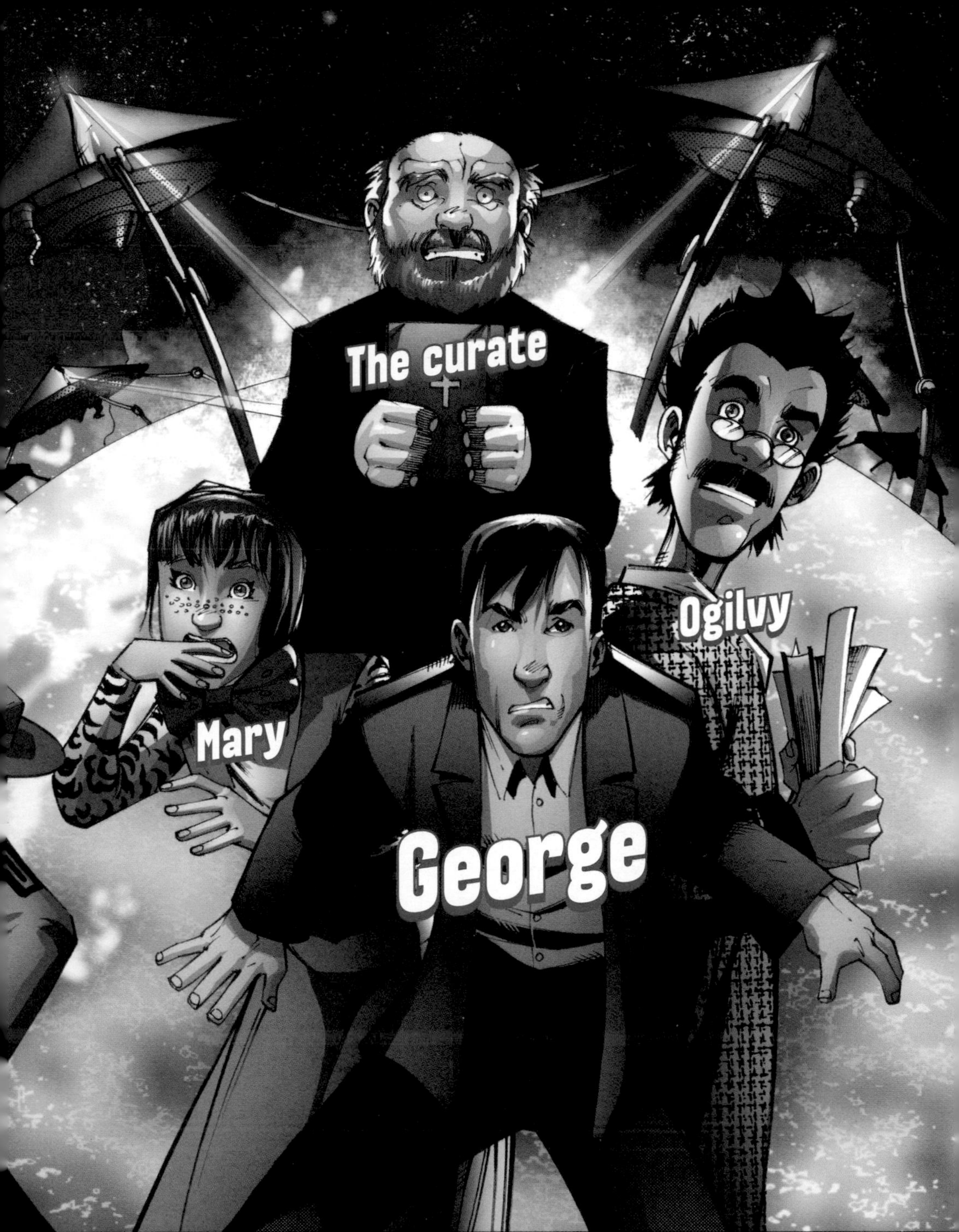
The curate
Ogilvy
Mary
George

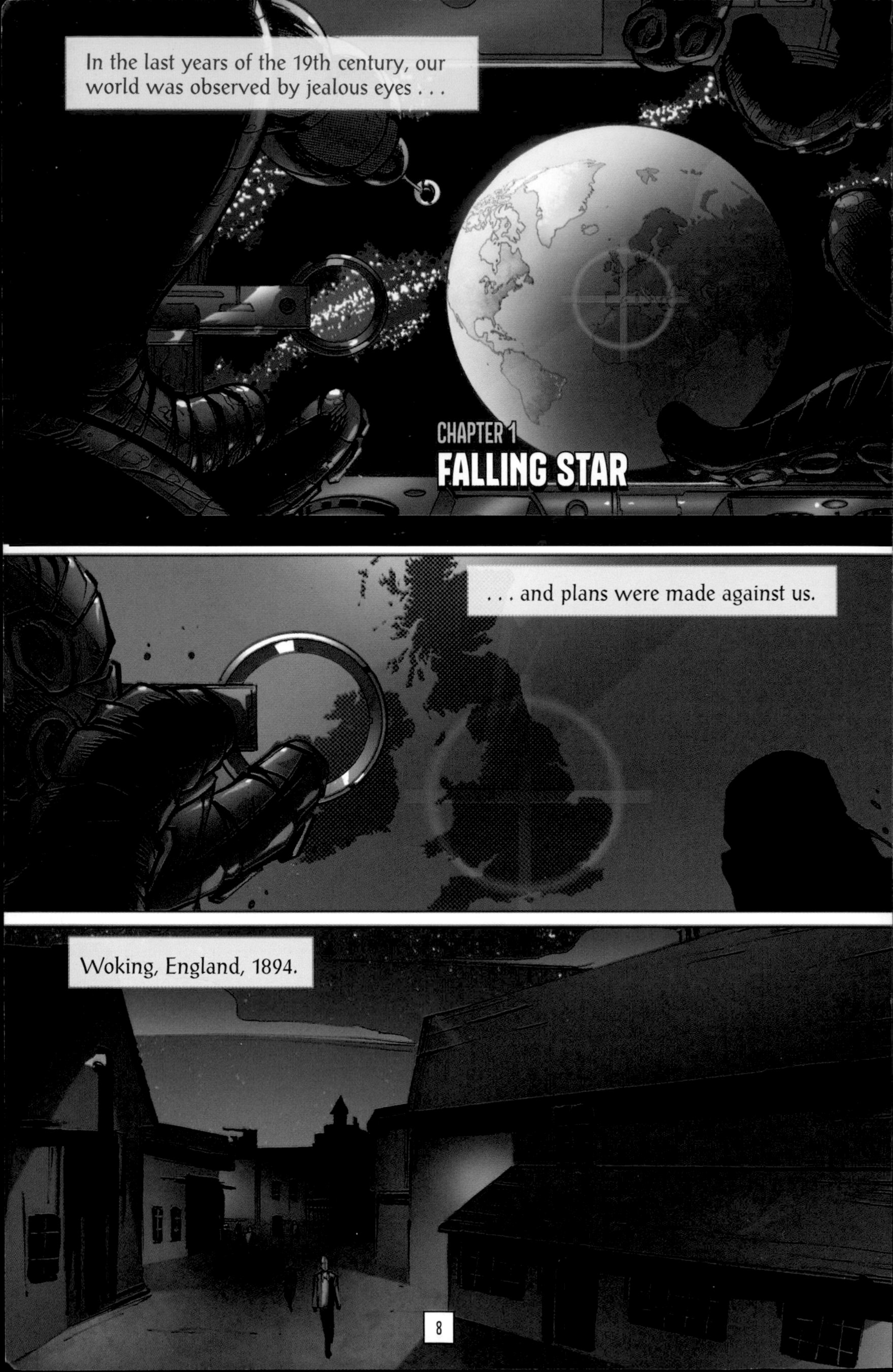
In the last years of the 19th century, our world was observed by jealous eyes . . .
CHAPTER 1
FALLING STAR
. . . and plans were made against us.
Woking, England, 1894.

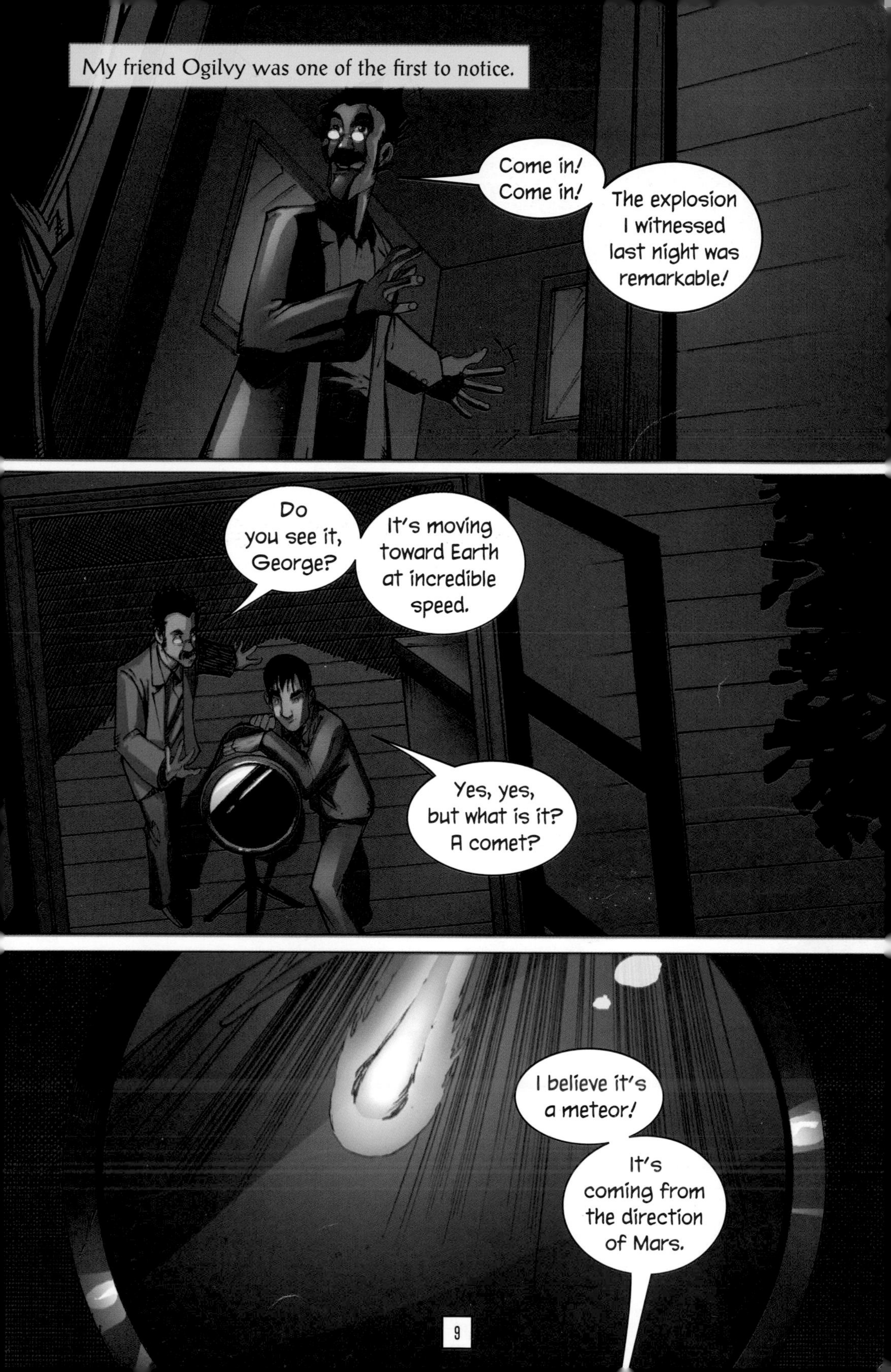
My friend Ogilvy was one of the first to notice.
Come in! Come in!
The explosion I witnessed last night was remarkable!
Do you see it, George?
It's moving toward Earth at incredible speed.
Yes, yes, but what is it? A comet?
I believe it's a meteor!
It's coming from the direction of Mars.

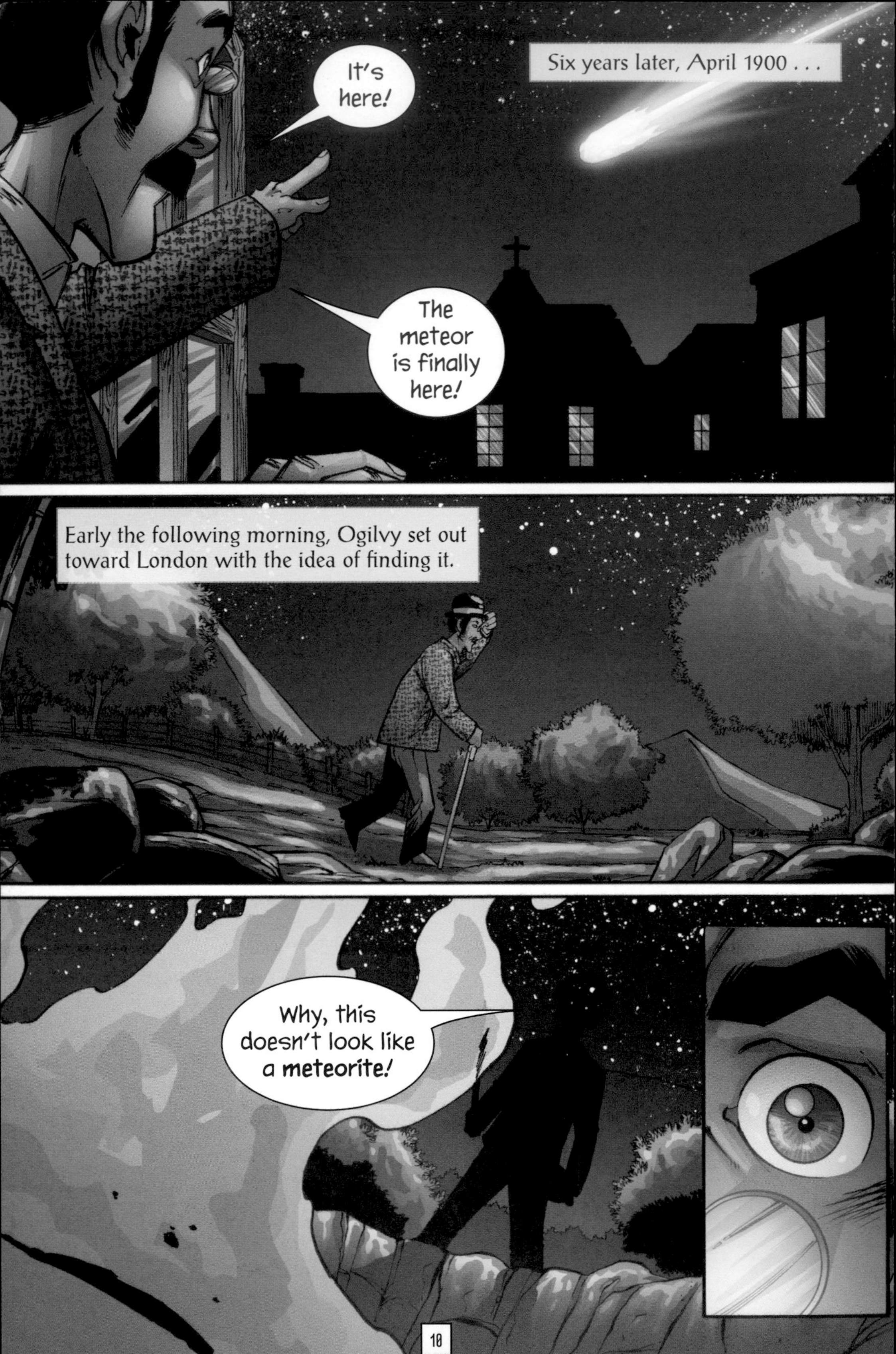
Six years later, April 1900 . . .
It's here!
The meteor is finally here!
Early the following morning, Ogilvy set out toward London with the idea of finding it.
Why, this doesn't look like a meteorite!

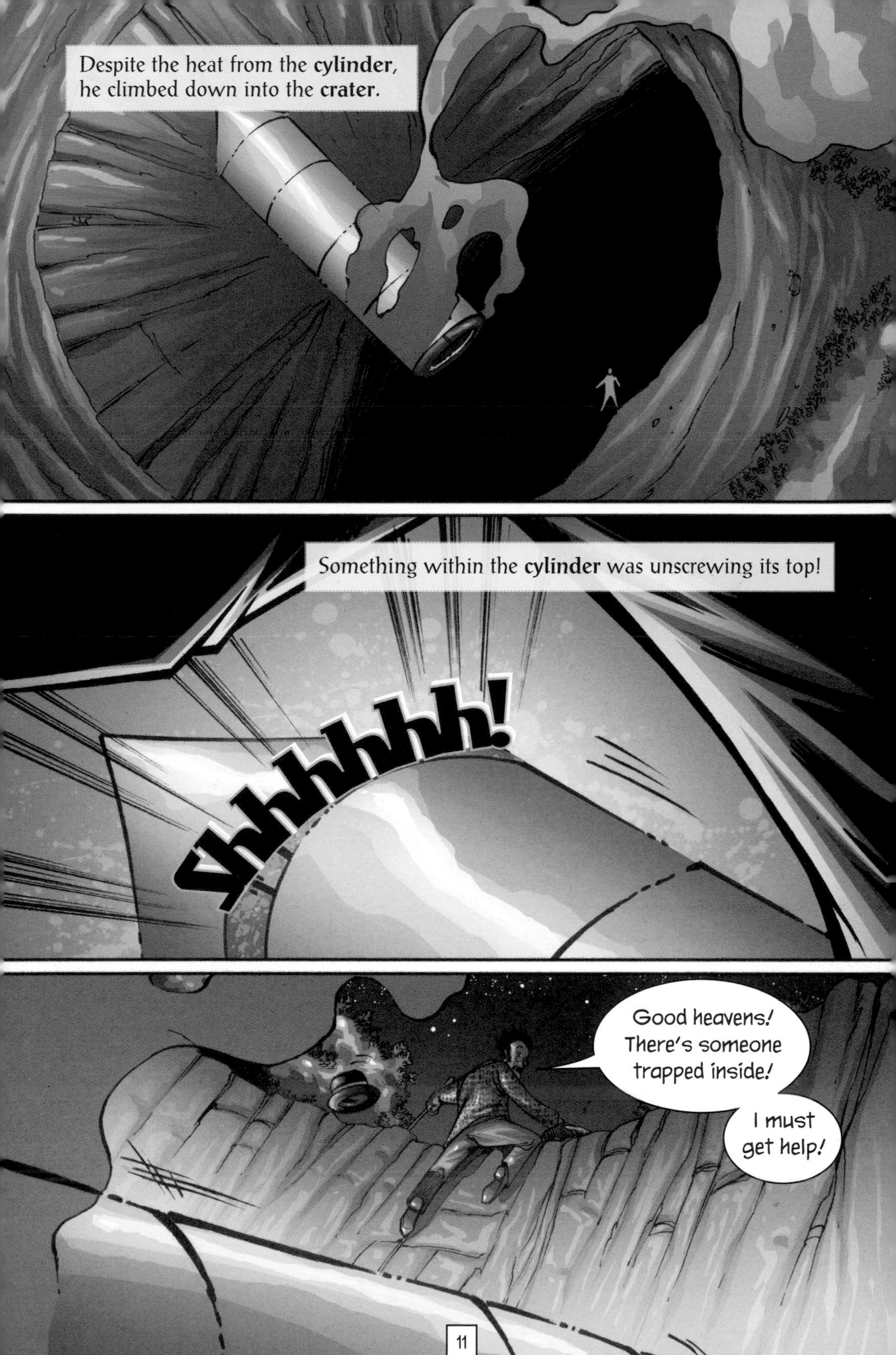
Despite the heat from the **cylinder**, he climbed down into the **crater**.
Something within the **cylinder** was unscrewing its top!
Shhhhhh!
Good heavens! There's someone trapped inside!
I must get help!

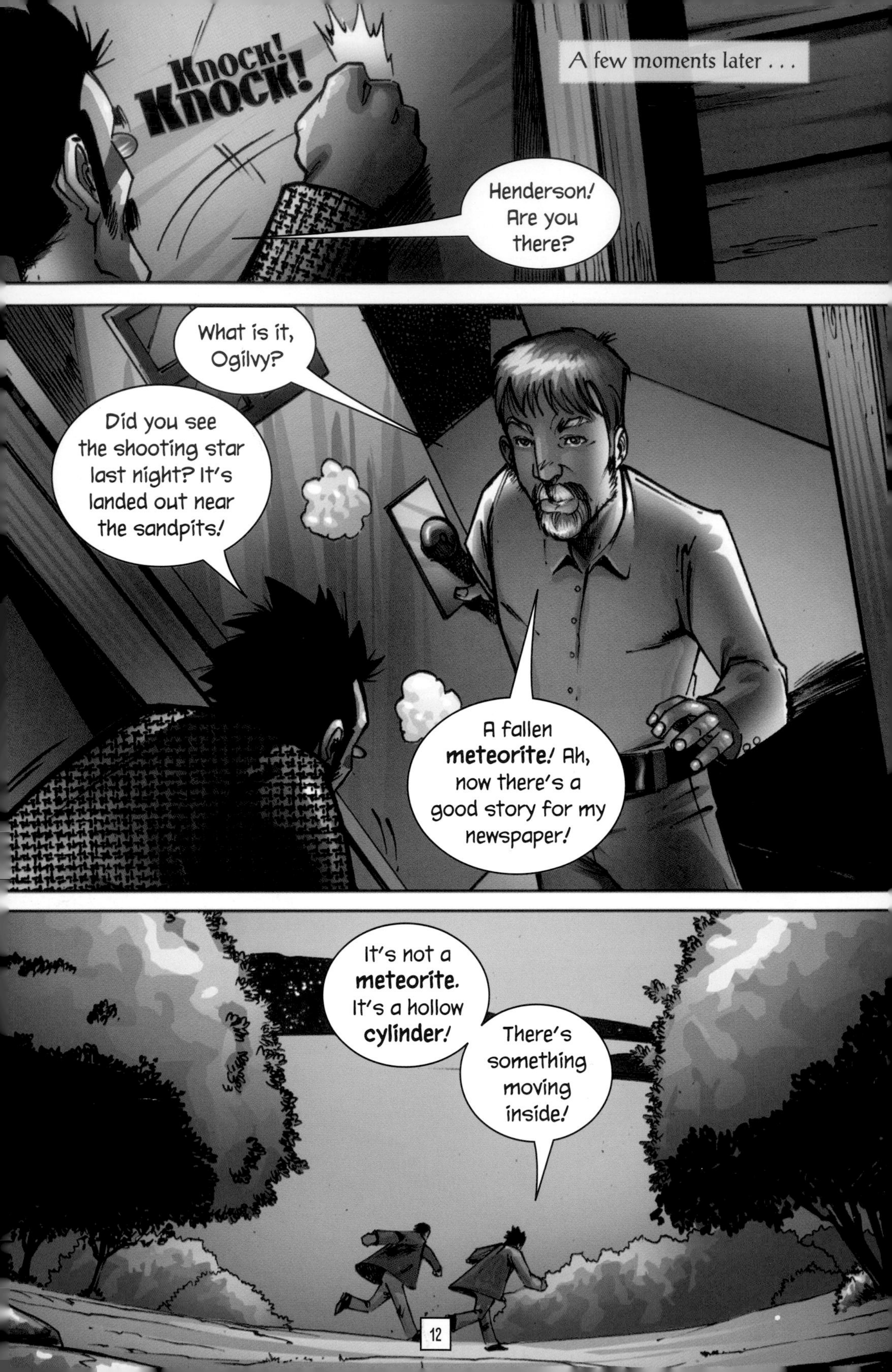

A few moments later . . .
KNOCK! KNOCK!
Henderson! Are you there?
What is it, Ogilvy?
Did you see the shooting star last night? It's landed out near the sandpits!
A fallen **meteorite**! Ah, now there's a good story for my newspaper!
It's not a **meteorite**. It's a hollow **cylinder**!
There's something moving inside!

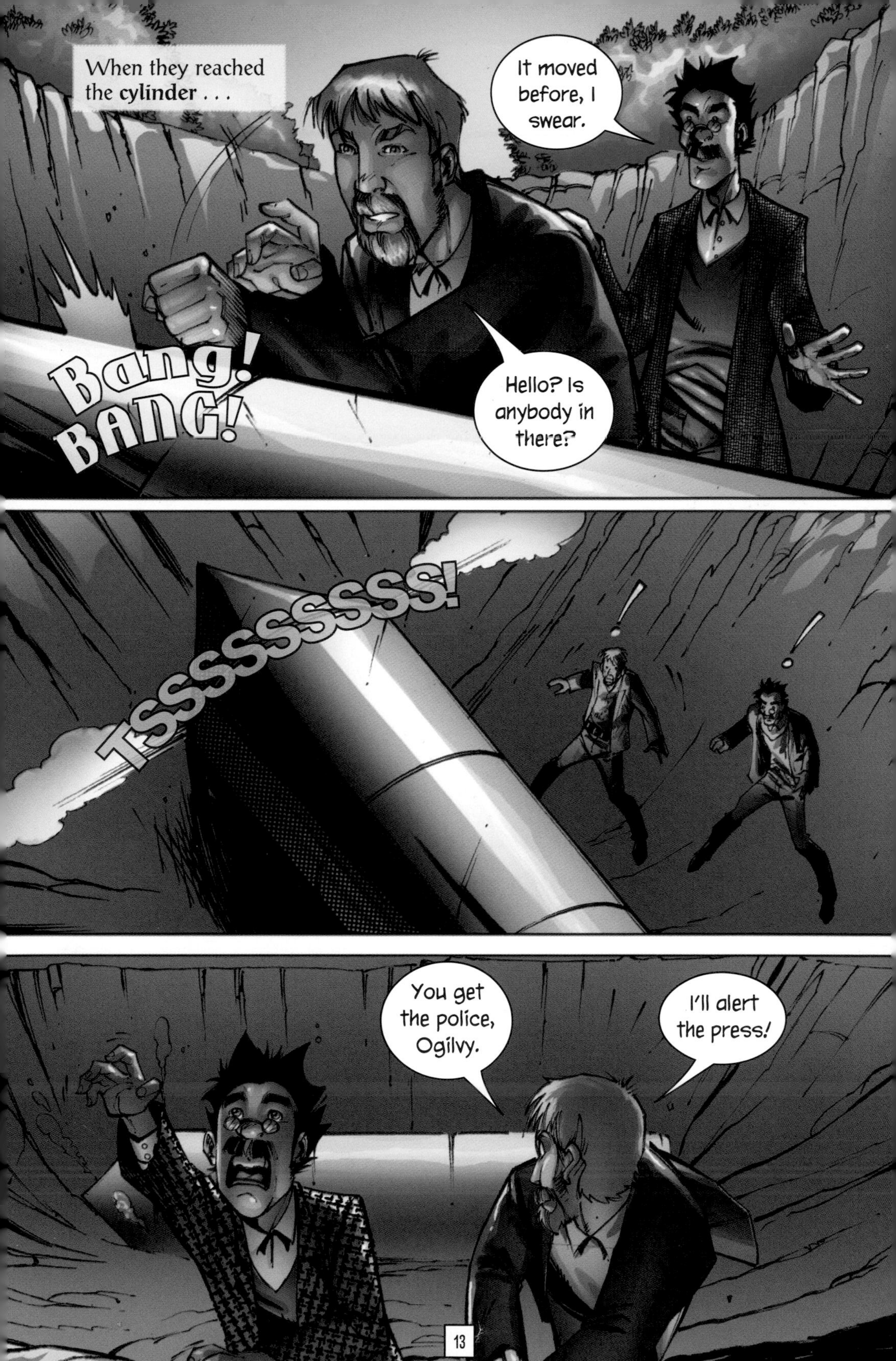
When they reached the **cylinder** . . .
It moved before, I swear.
Bang! BANG!
Hello? Is anybody in there?
TSSSSSSSSS!
You get the police, Ogilvy.
I'll alert the press!

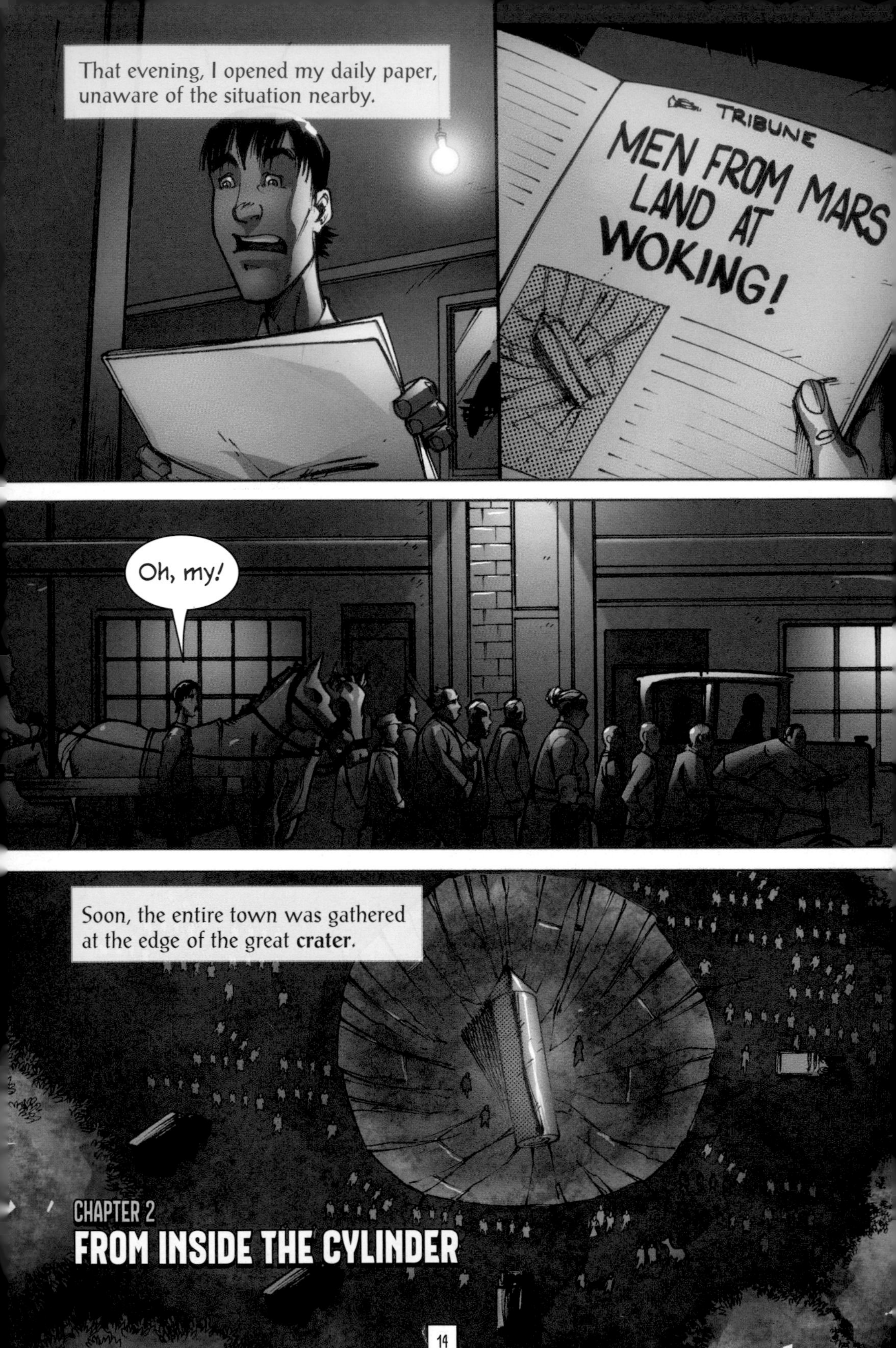
That evening, I opened my daily paper, unaware of the situation nearby.
TRIBUNE
MEN FROM MARS LAND AT WOKING!
Oh, my!
Soon, the entire town was gathered at the edge of the great **crater**.
CHAPTER 2
FROM INSIDE THE CYLINDER

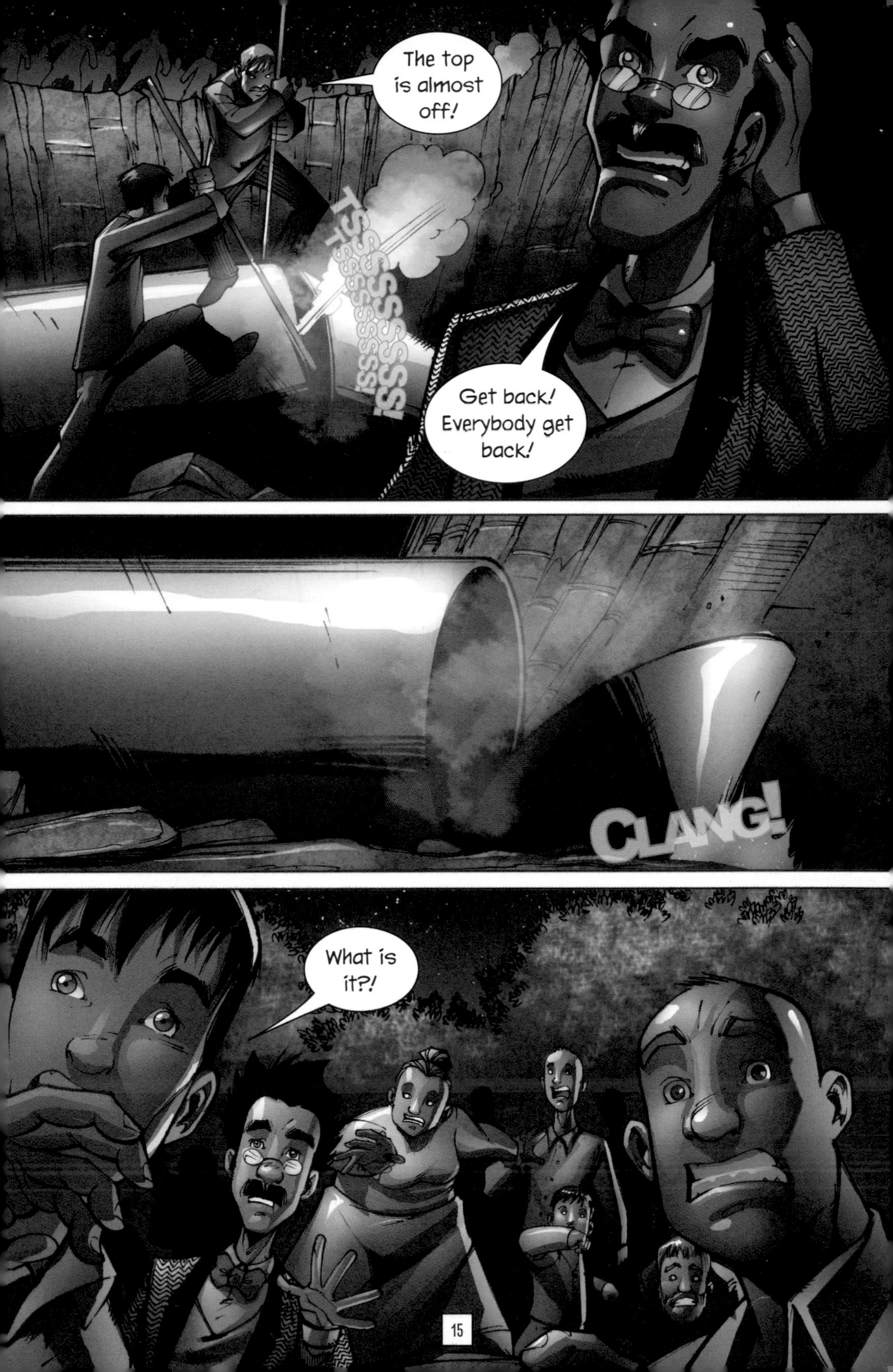

The top is almost off!
TSSSSSSSS!
Get back! Everybody get back!
CLANG!
What is it?!

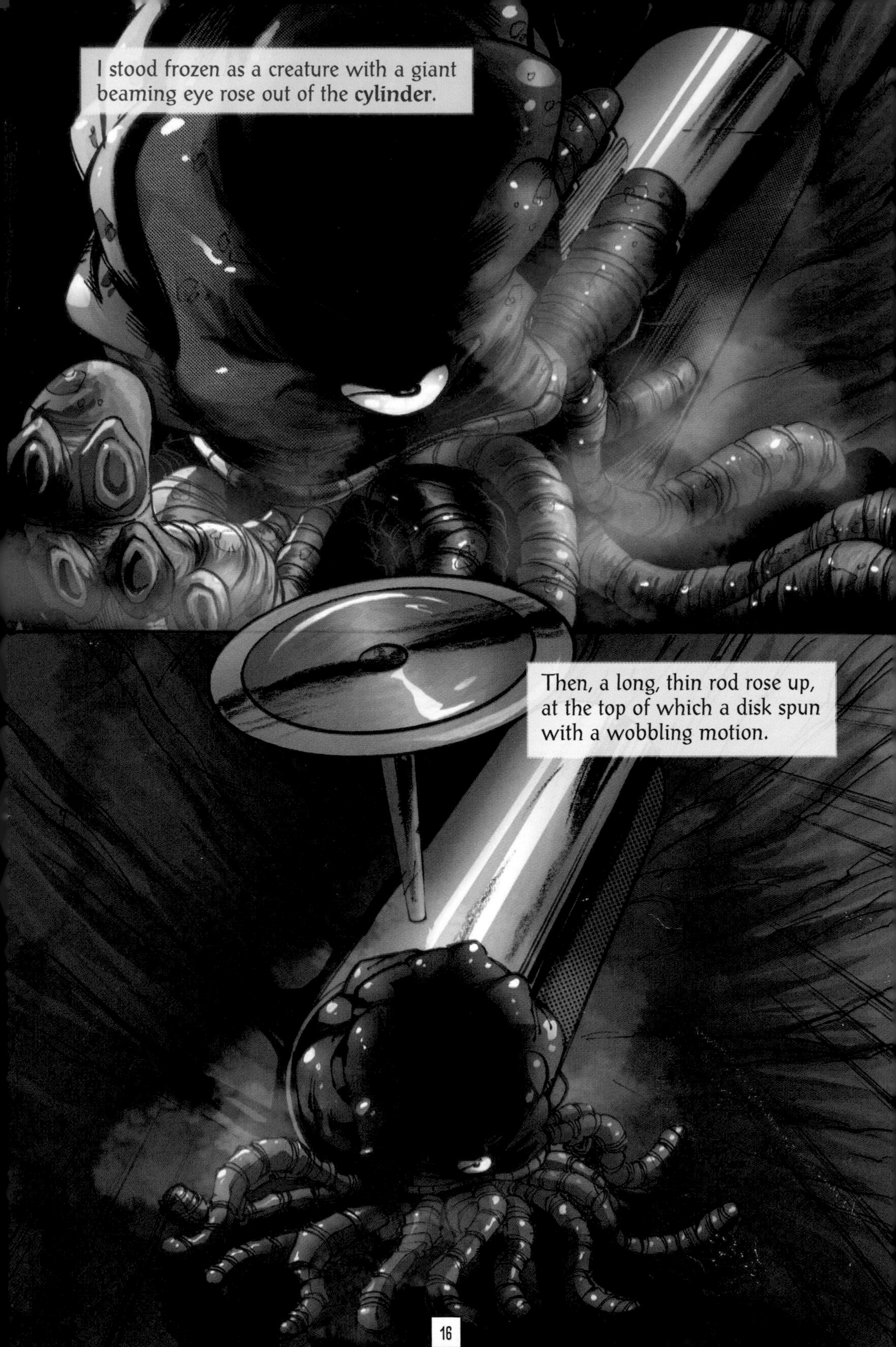
I stood frozen as a creature with a giant beaming eye rose out of the **cylinder**.
Then, a long, thin rod rose up, at the top of which a disk spun with a wobbling motion.

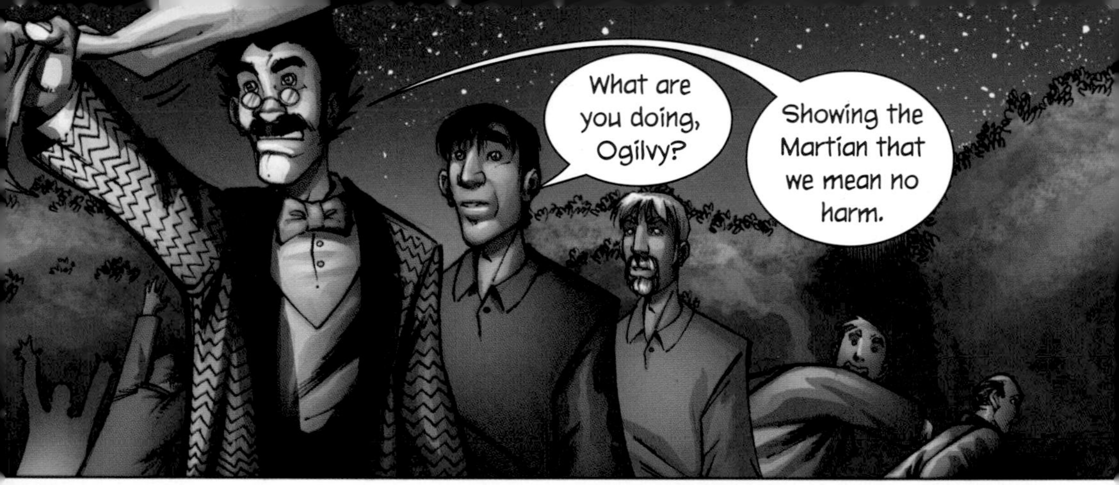
What are you doing, Ogilvy?
Showing the Martian that we mean no harm.

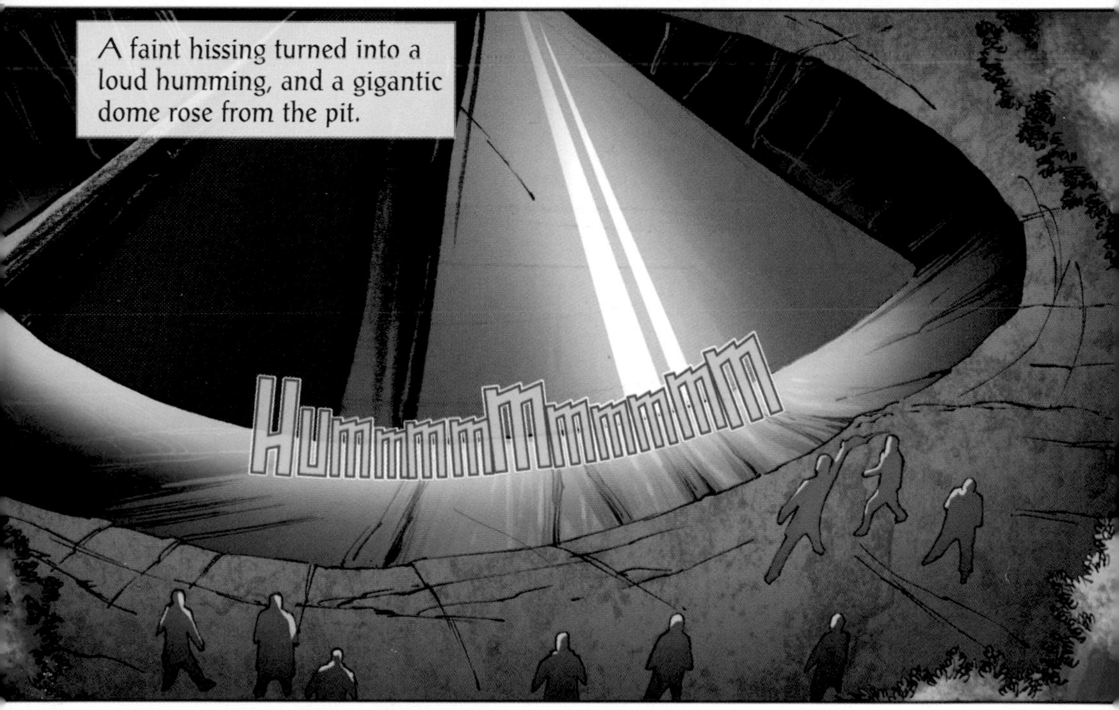
A faint hissing turned into a loud humming, and a gigantic dome rose from the pit.
HUmmmmMmmmmM

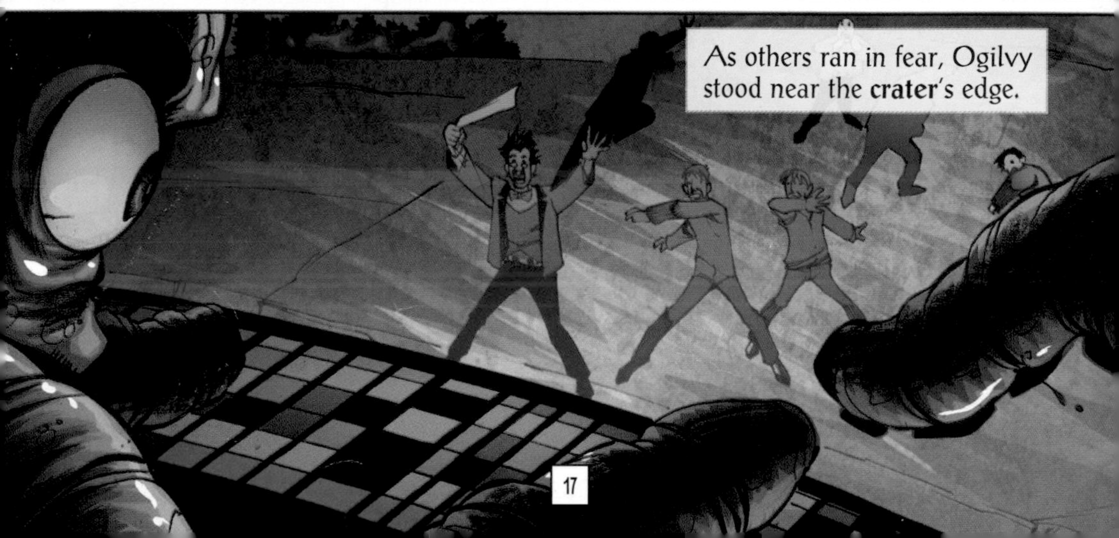
As others ran in fear, Ogilvy stood near the **crater**'s edge.

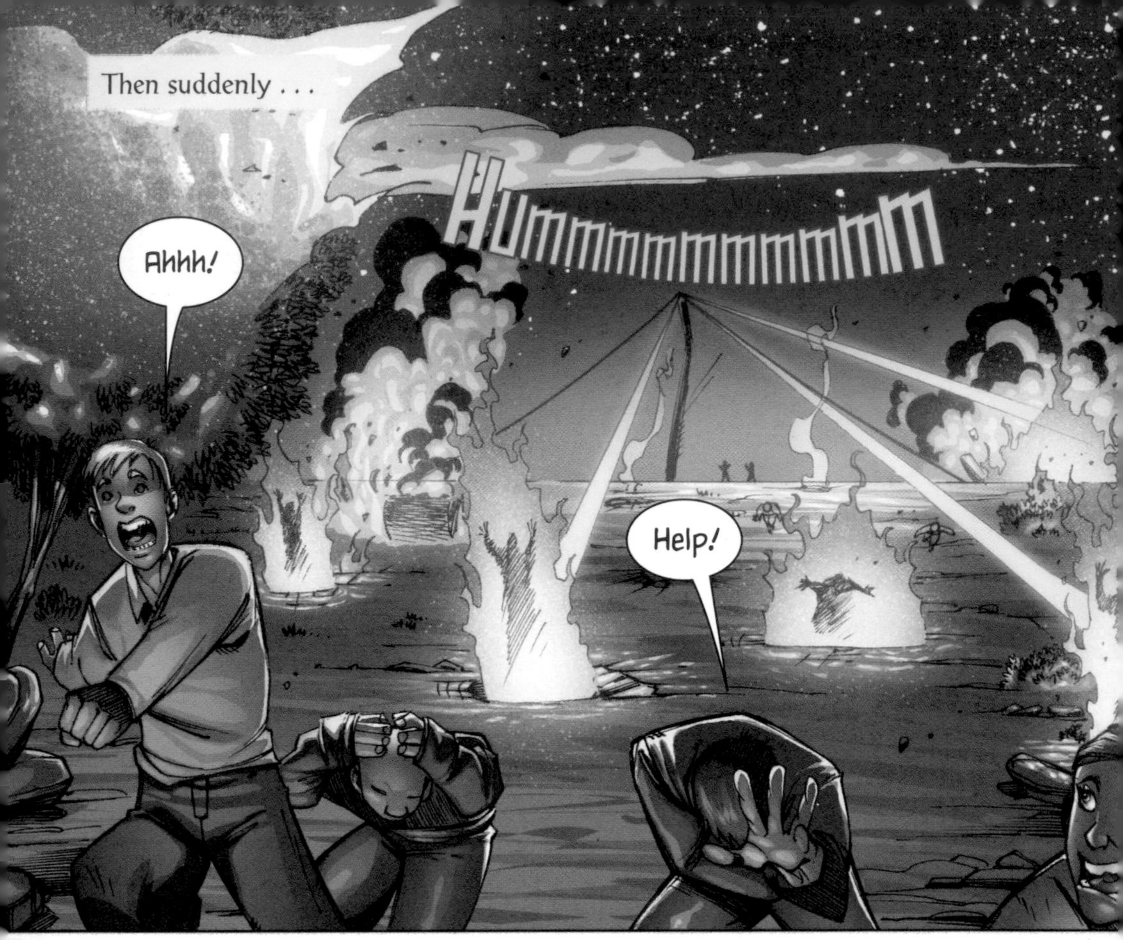
Then suddenly . . .
HUMMMMMMMMMMM
Ahhh!
Help!

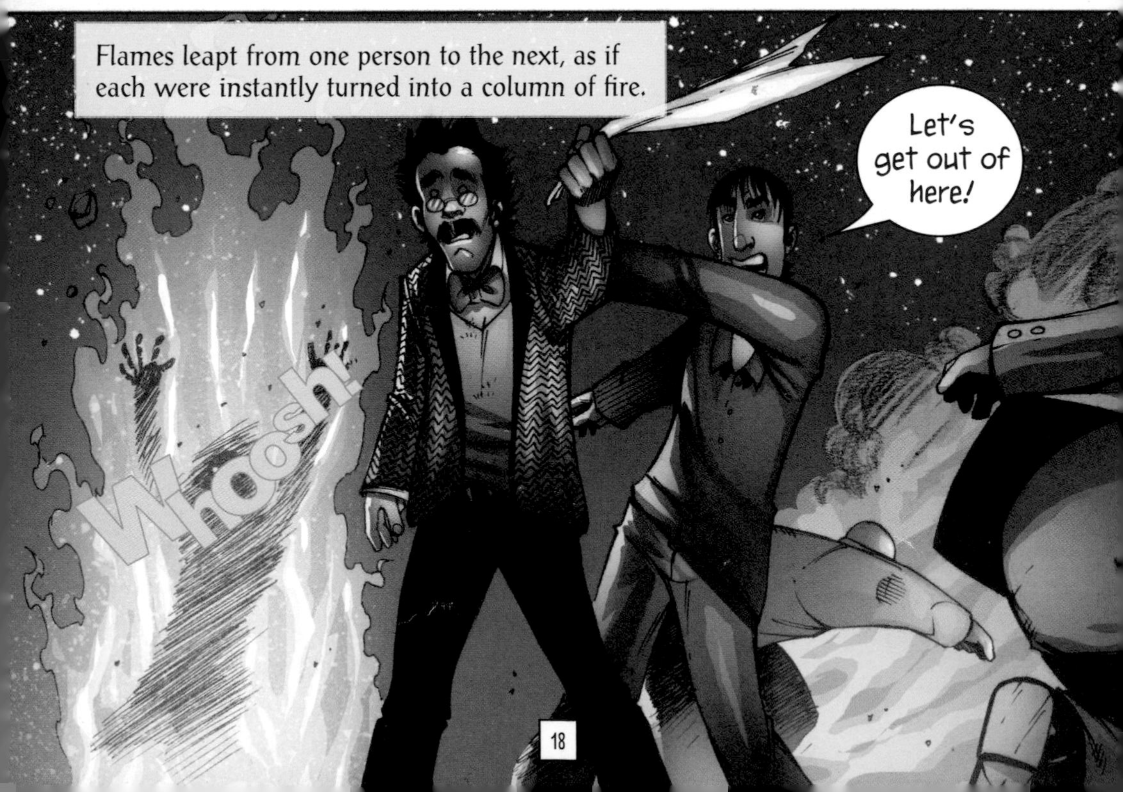
Flames leapt from one person to the next, as if each were instantly turned into a column of fire.
Let's get out of here!
Whoosh!

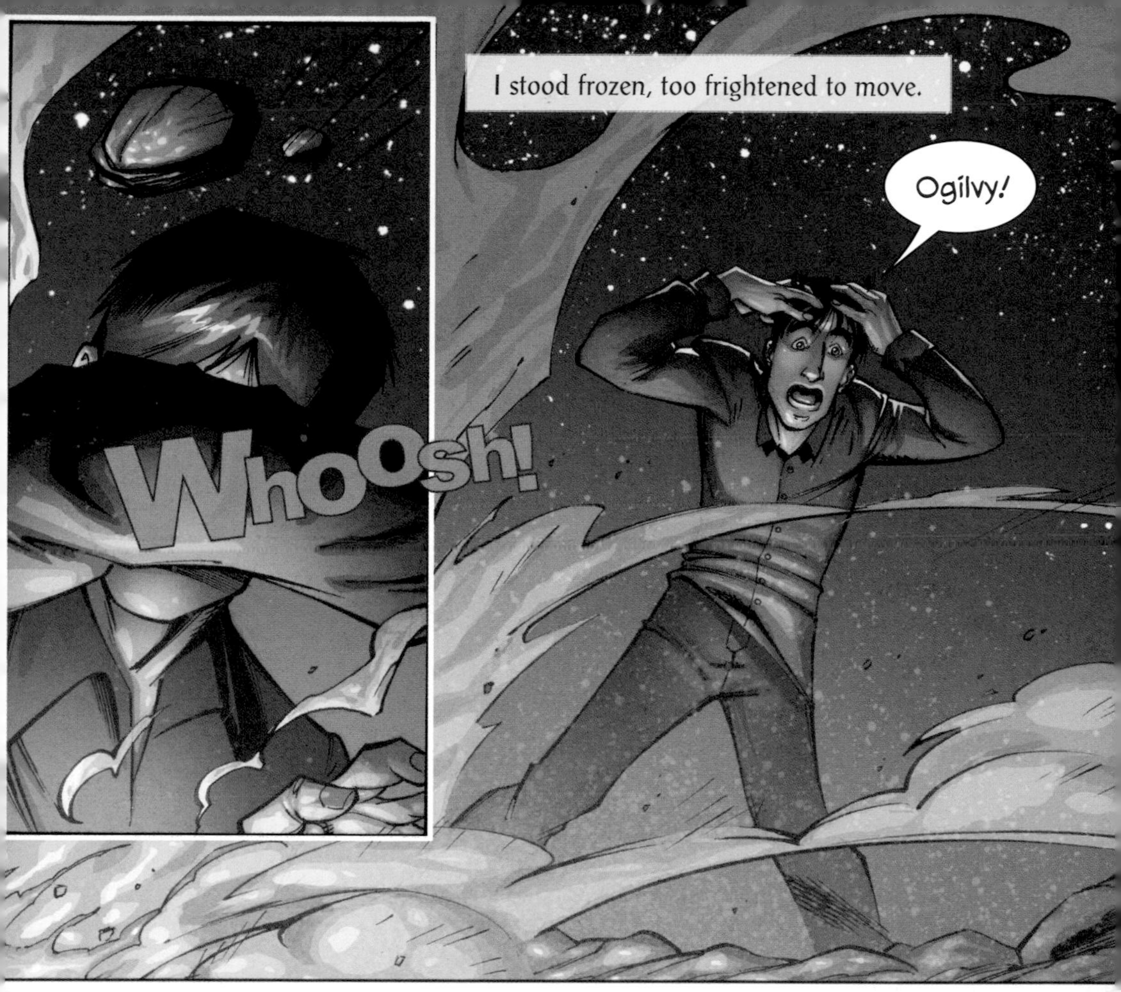
I stood frozen, too frightened to move.
Ogilvy!
WhoOsh!

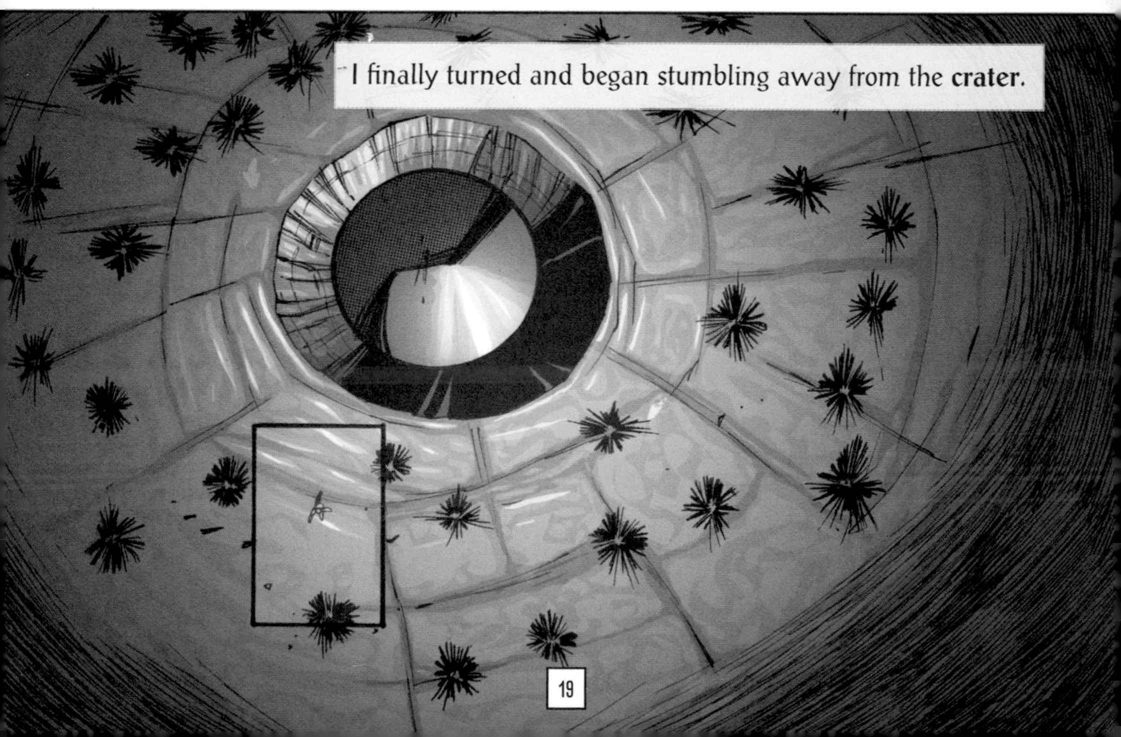
I finally turned and began stumbling away from the **crater**.

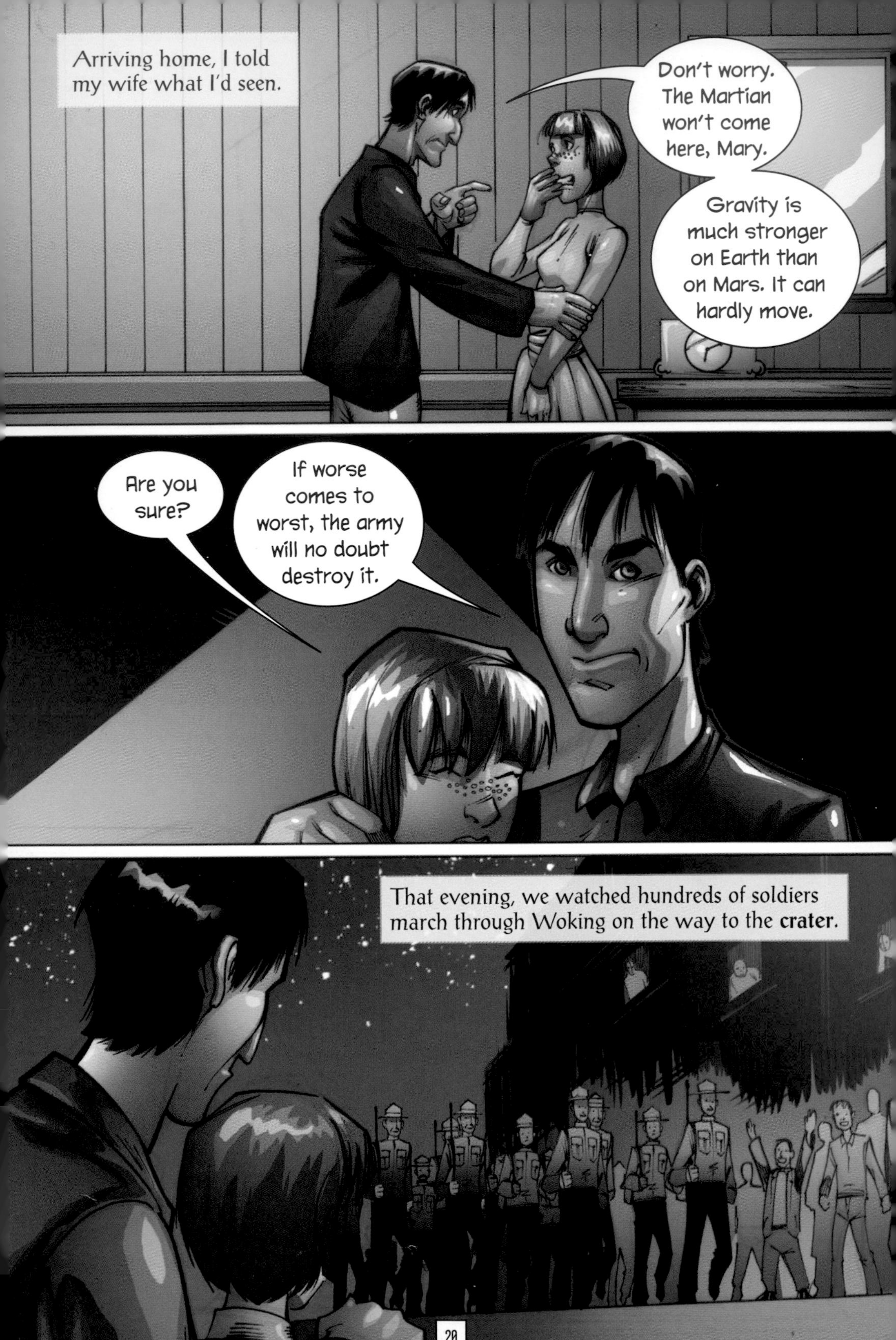
Arriving home, I told my wife what I'd seen.
Don't worry. The Martian won't come here, Mary.
Gravity is much stronger on Earth than on Mars. It can hardly move.
Are you sure?
If worse comes to worst, the army will no doubt destroy it.
That evening, we watched hundreds of soldiers march through Woking on the way to the **crater**.

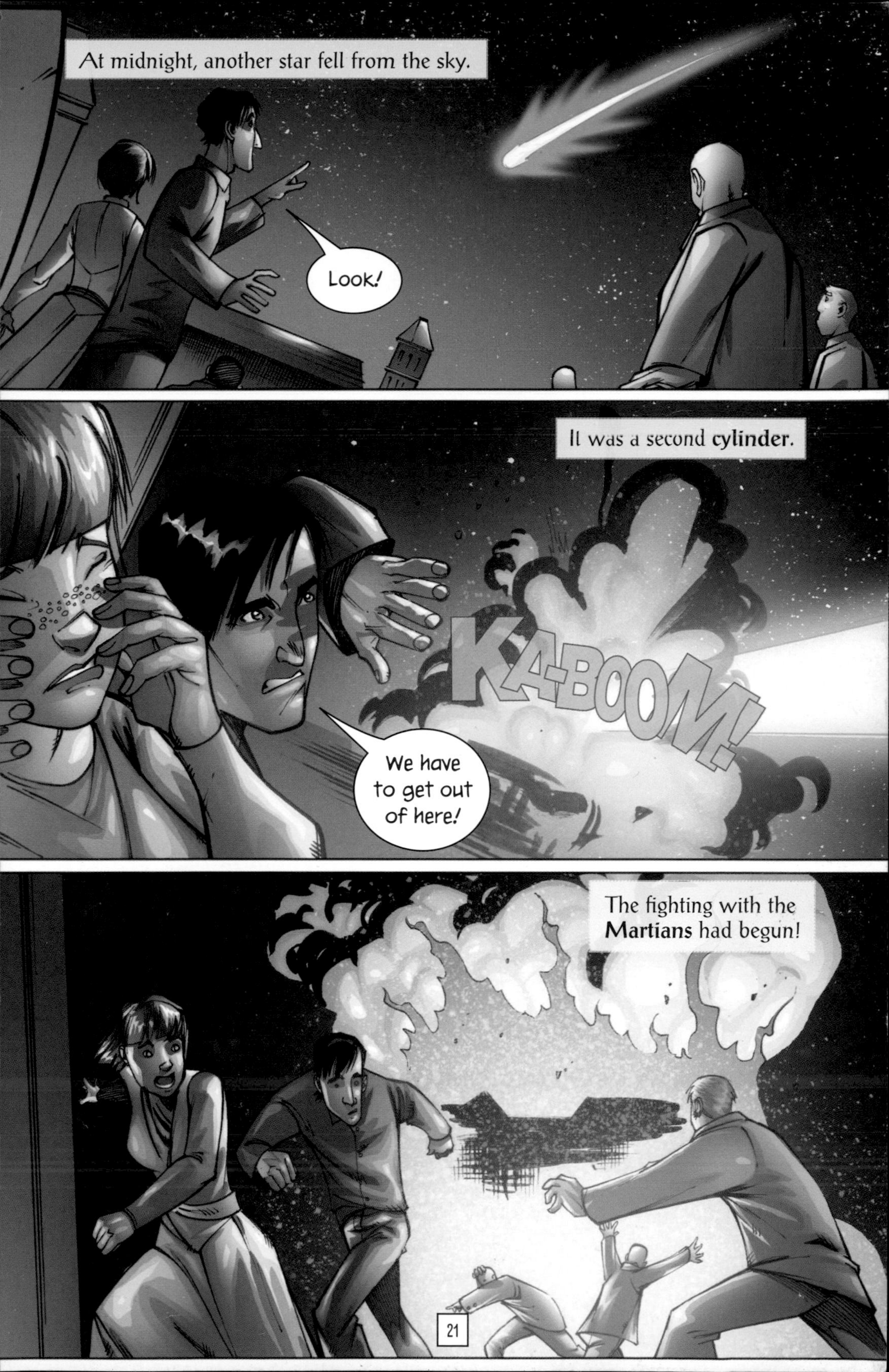
At midnight, another star fell from the sky.
Look!
It was a second **cylinder**.
KA-BOOM!
We have to get out of here!
The fighting with the **Martians** had begun!

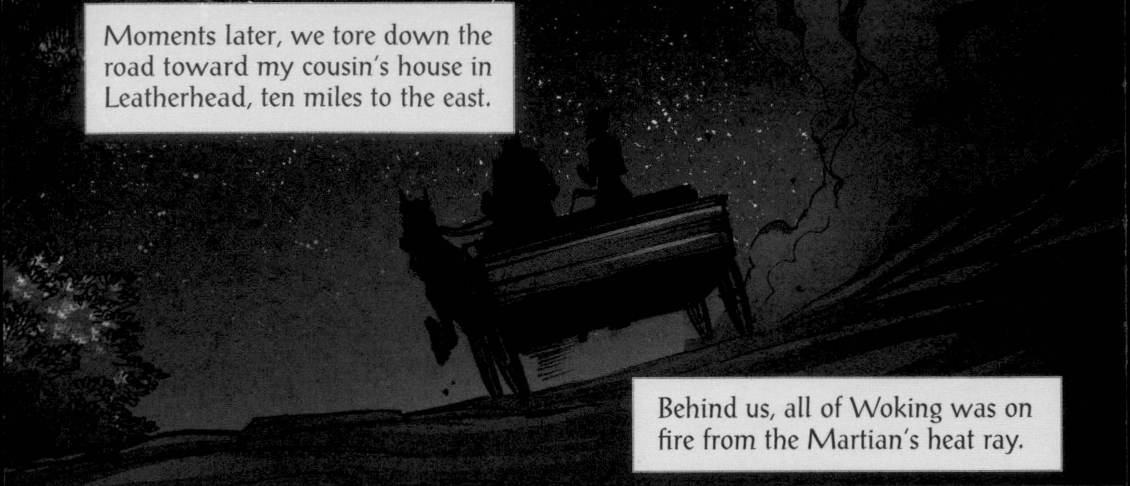
Moments later, we tore down the road toward my cousin's house in Leatherhead, ten miles to the east.
Behind us, all of Woking was on fire from the Martian's heat ray.

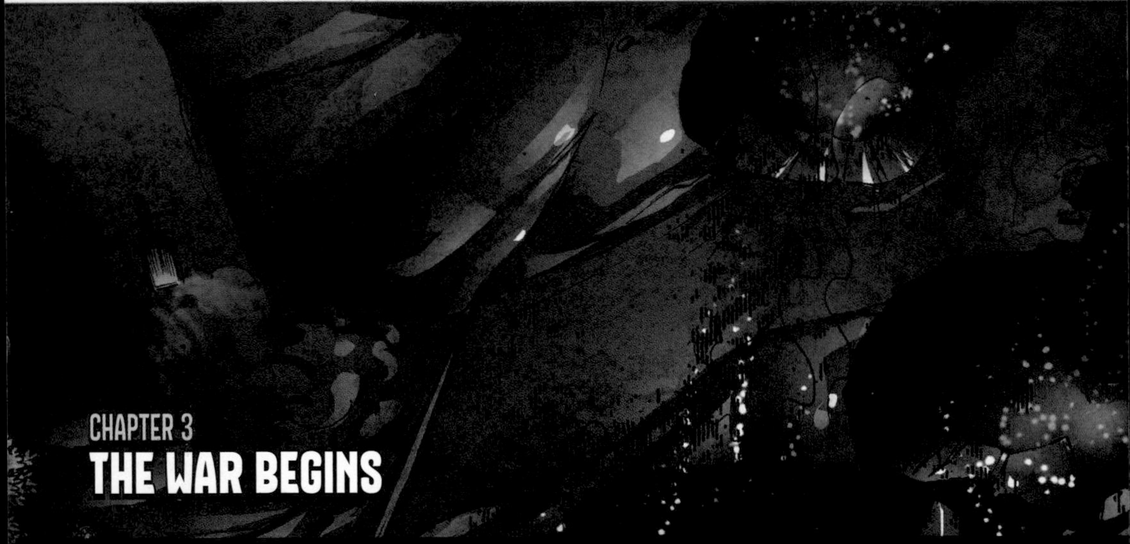

CHAPTER 3
THE WAR BEGINS

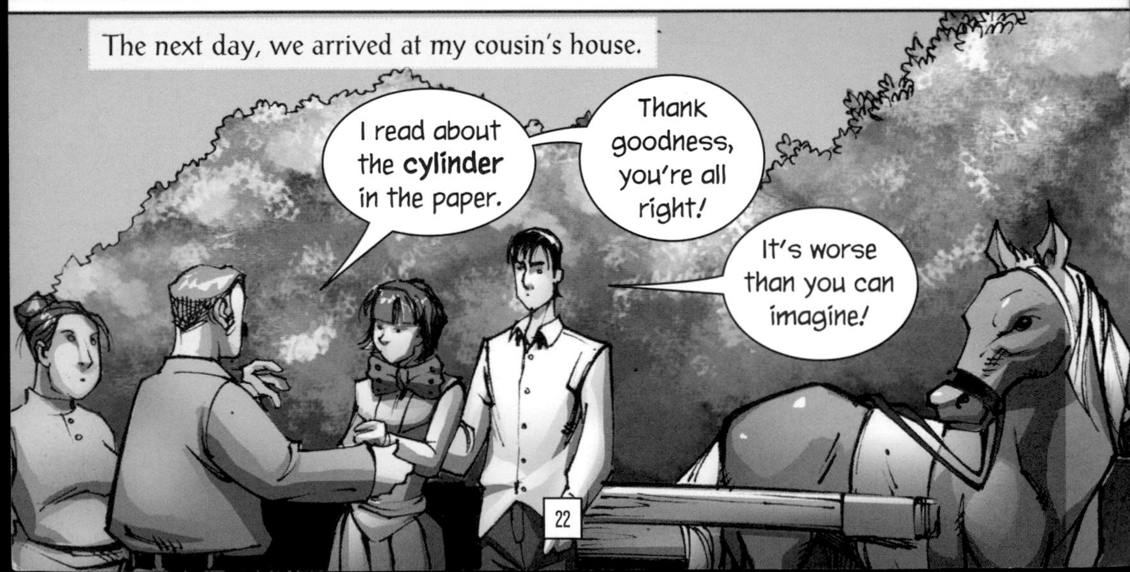
The next day, we arrived at my cousin's house.
Thank goodness, you're all right!
I read about the **cylinder** in the paper.
It's worse than you can imagine!

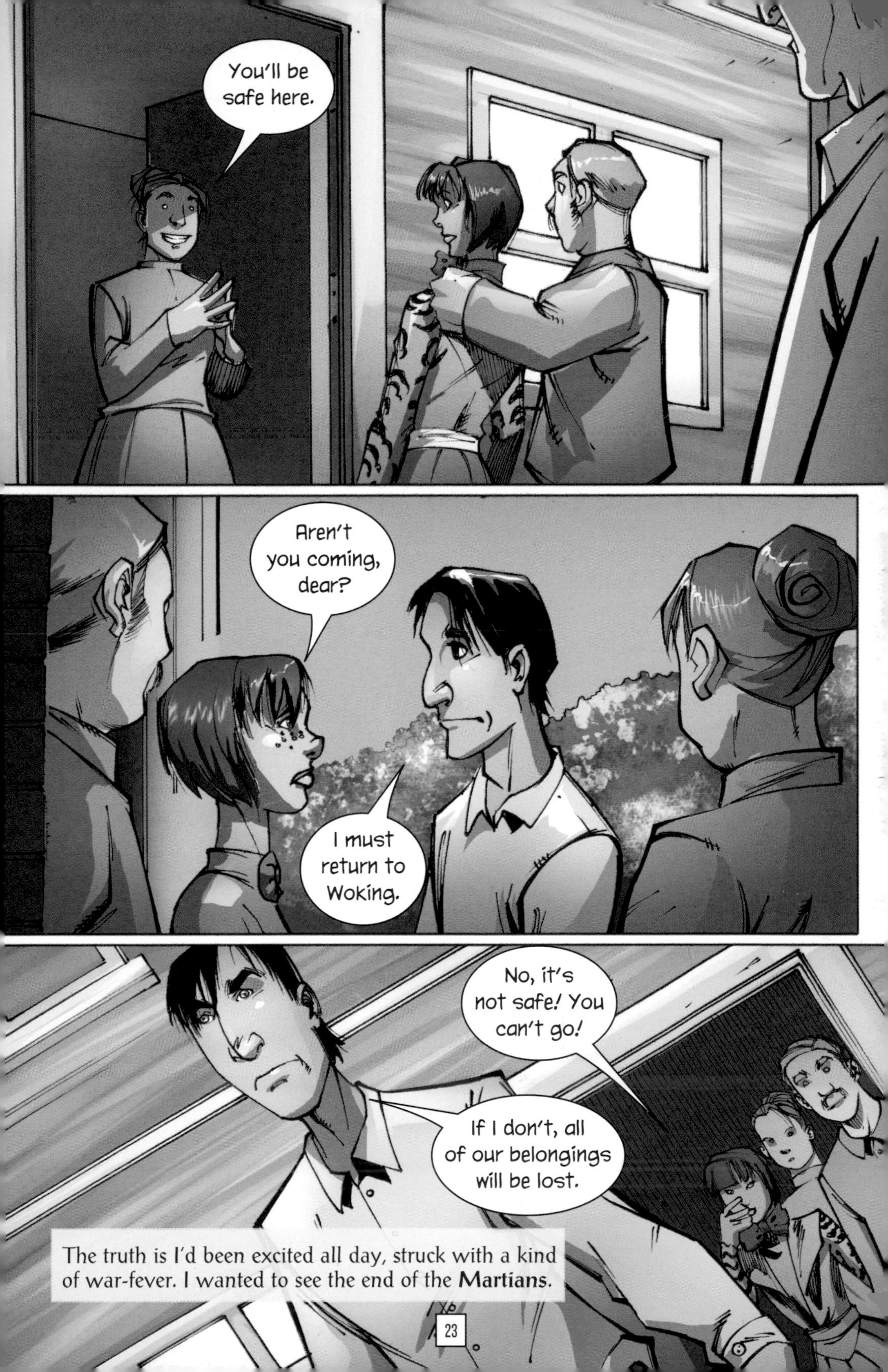
You'll be safe here.
Aren't you coming, dear?
I must return to Woking.
No, it's not safe! You can't go!
If I don't, all of our belongings will be lost.
The truth is I'd been excited all day, struck with a kind of war-fever. I wanted to see the end of the **Martians**.

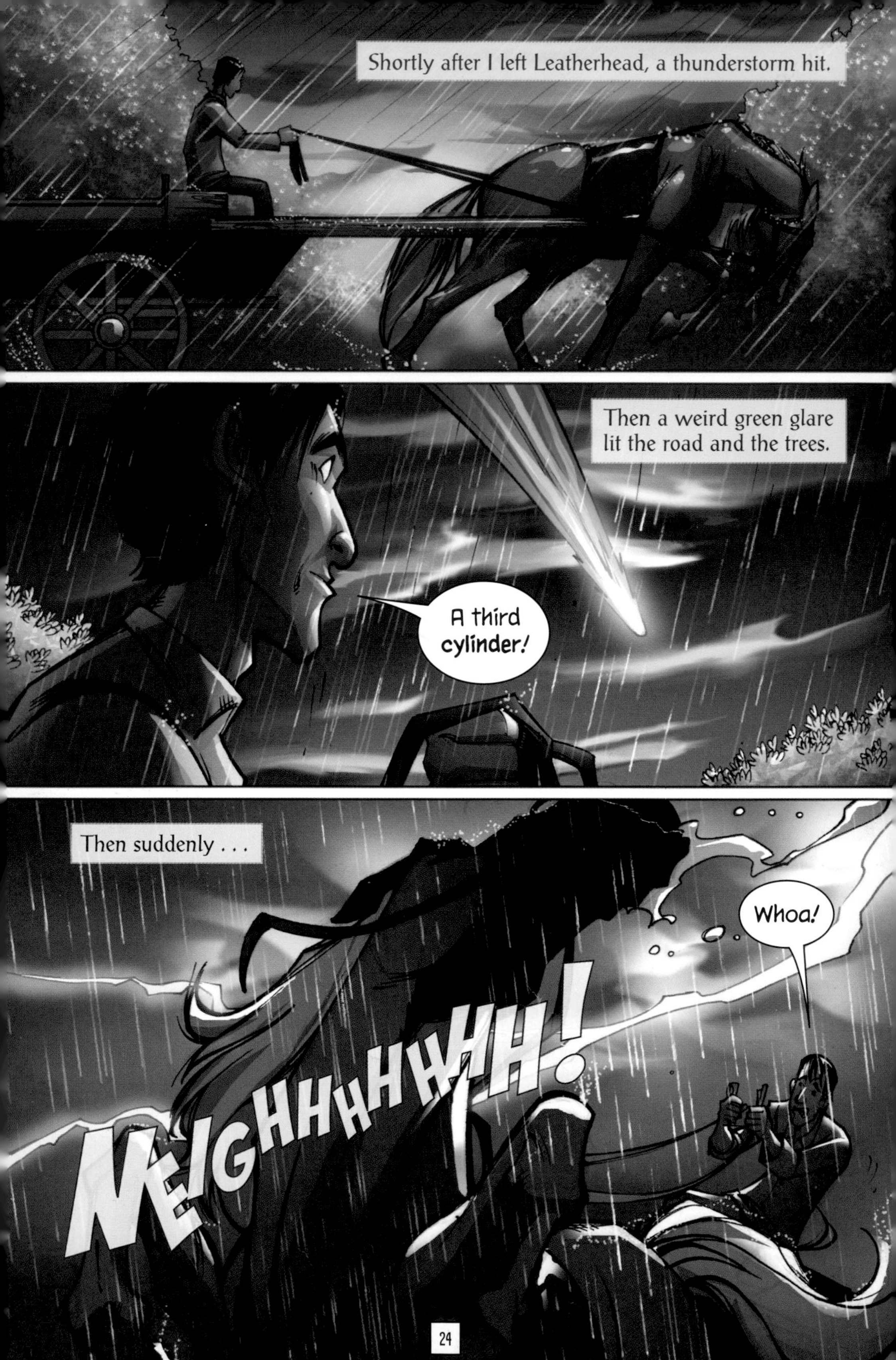
Shortly after I left Leatherhead, a thunderstorm hit.
Then a weird green glare lit the road and the trees.
A third cylinder!
Then suddenly . . .
Whoa!
NEIGHHHHHHH!

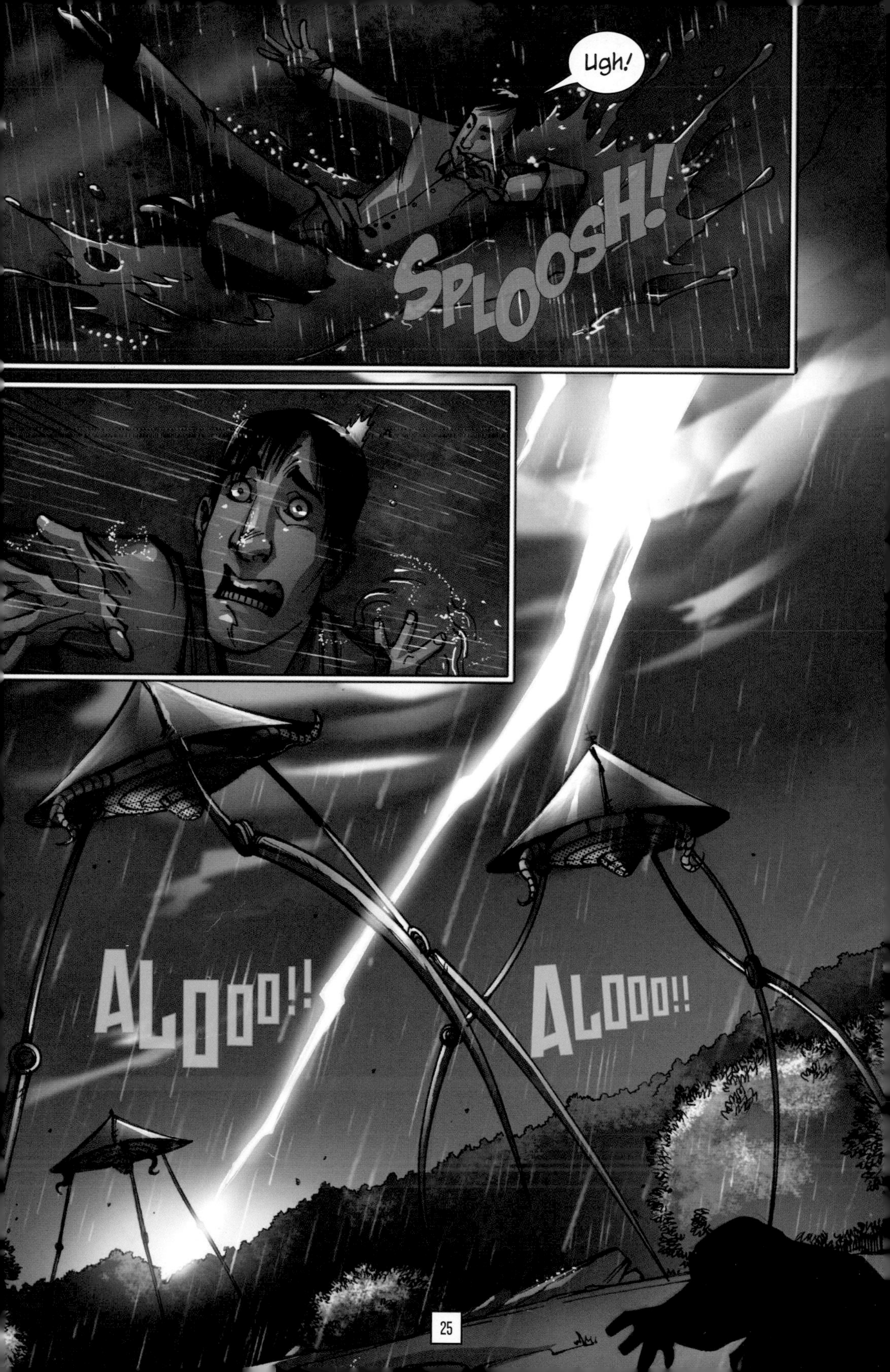
Ugh!
SPLOOSH!
ALOOO!!
ALOOO!!

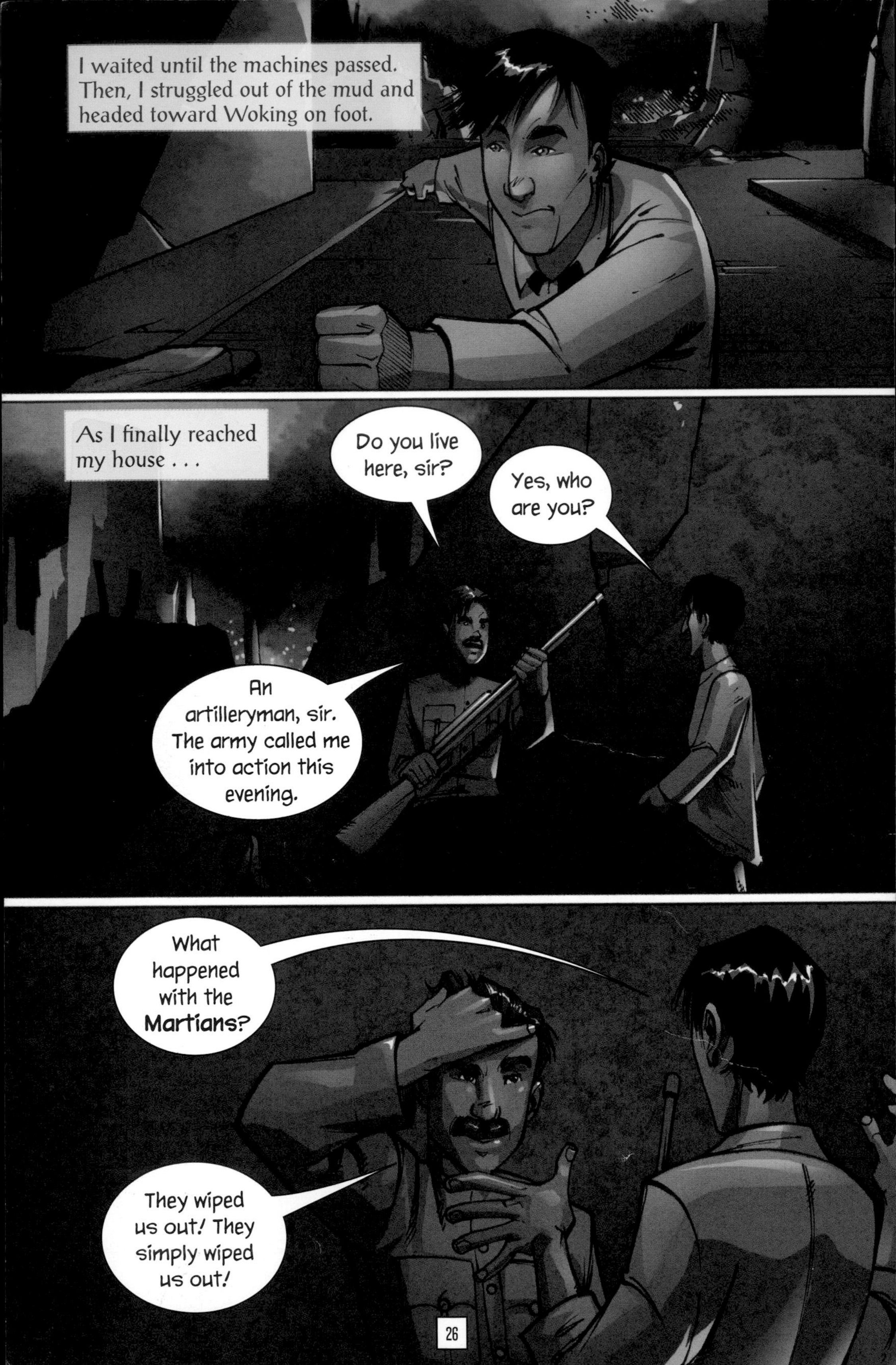
I waited until the machines passed. Then, I struggled out of the mud and headed toward Woking on foot.
As I finally reached my house . . .
Do you live here, sir?
Yes, who are you?
An artilleryman, sir. The army called me into action this evening.
What happened with the Martians?
They wiped us out! They simply wiped us out!

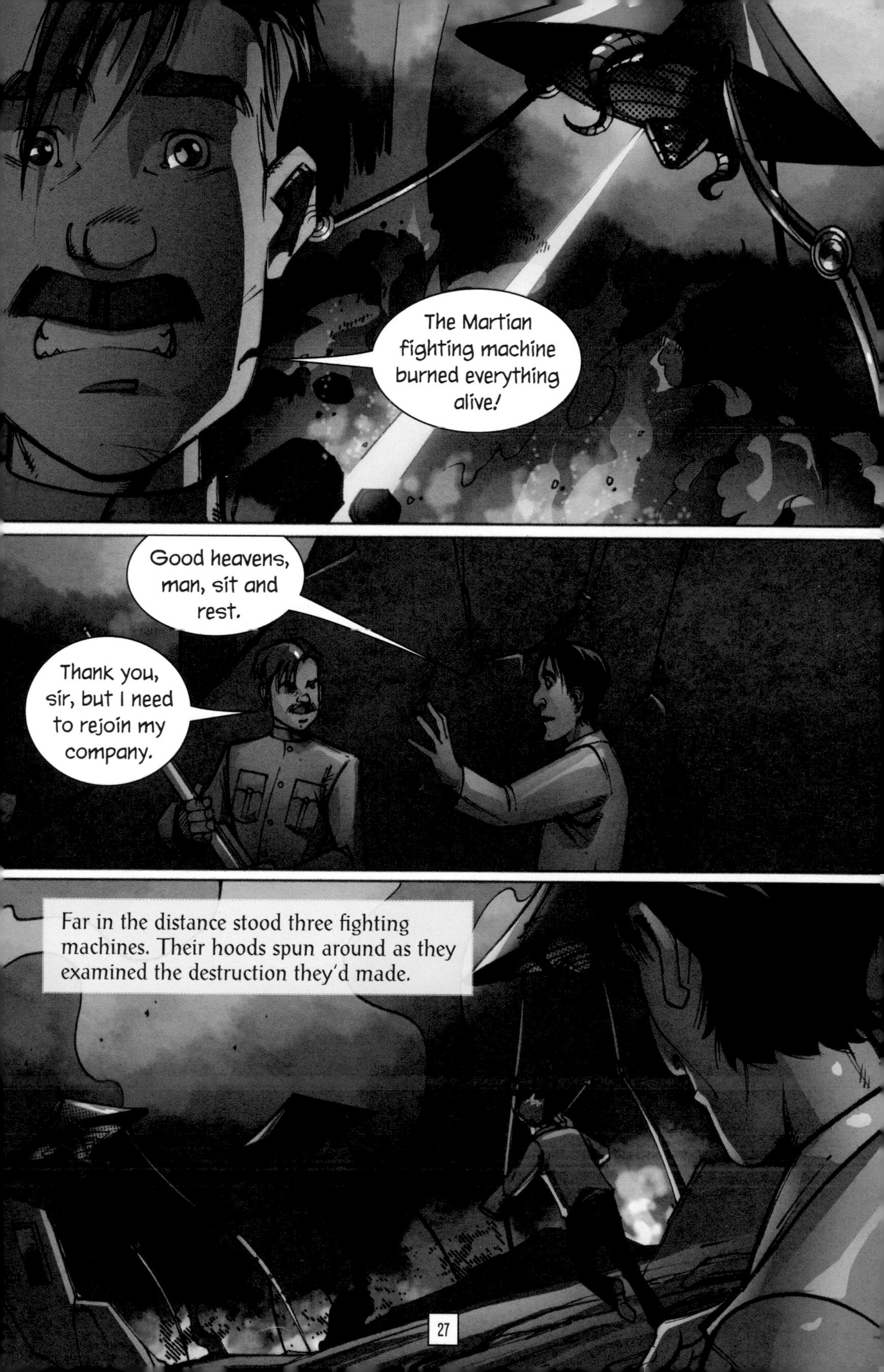
The Martian fighting machine burned everything alive!
Good heavens, man, sit and rest.
Thank you, sir, but I need to rejoin my company.
Far in the distance stood three fighting machines. Their hoods spun around as they examined the destruction they'd made.

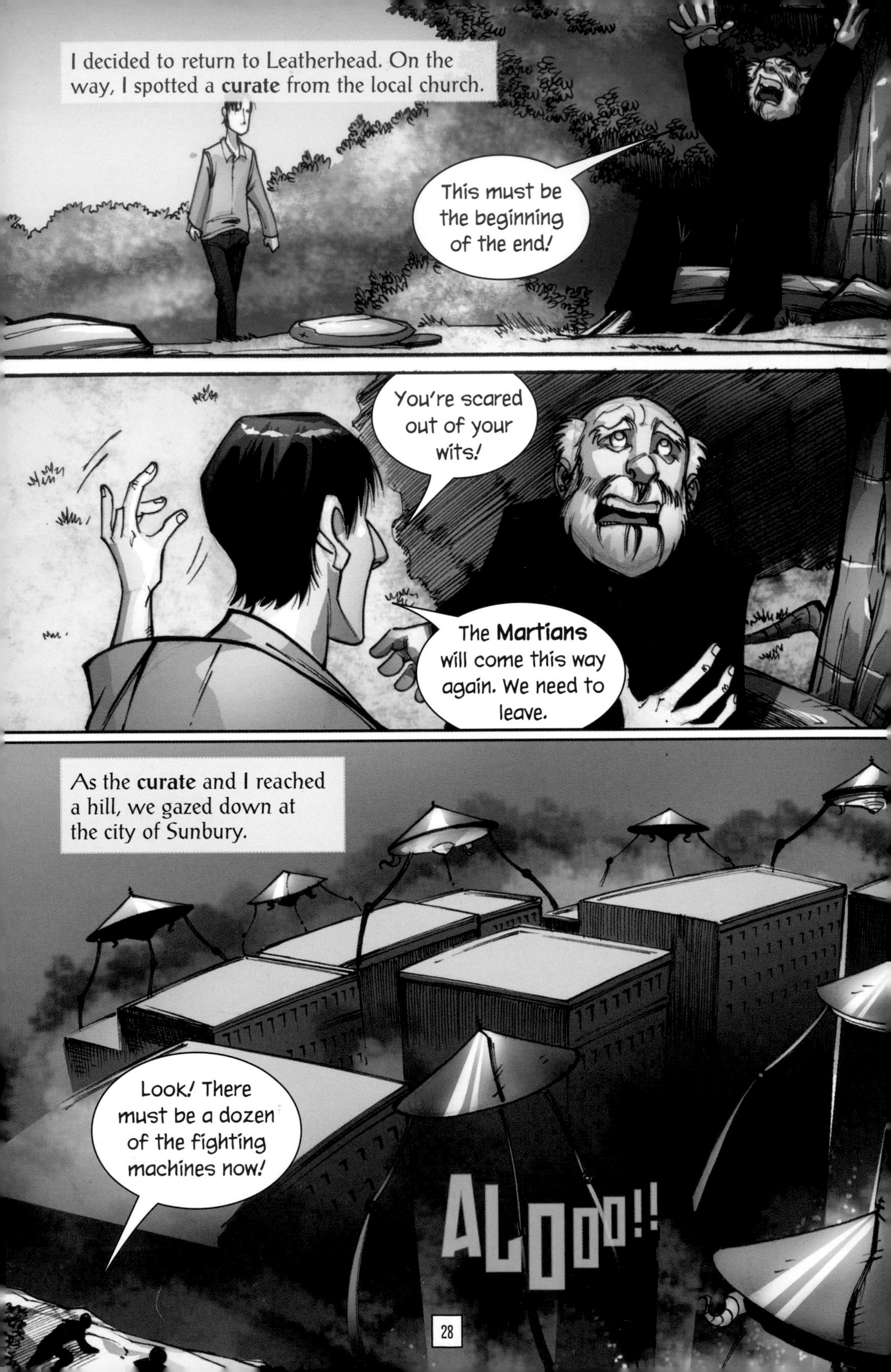
I decided to return to Leatherhead. On the way, I spotted a **curate** from the local church.
This must be the beginning of the end!
You're scared out of your wits!
The **Martians** will come this way again. We need to leave.
As the **curate** and I reached a hill, we gazed down at the city of Sunbury.
Look! There must be a dozen of the fighting machines now!
ALOOO!!

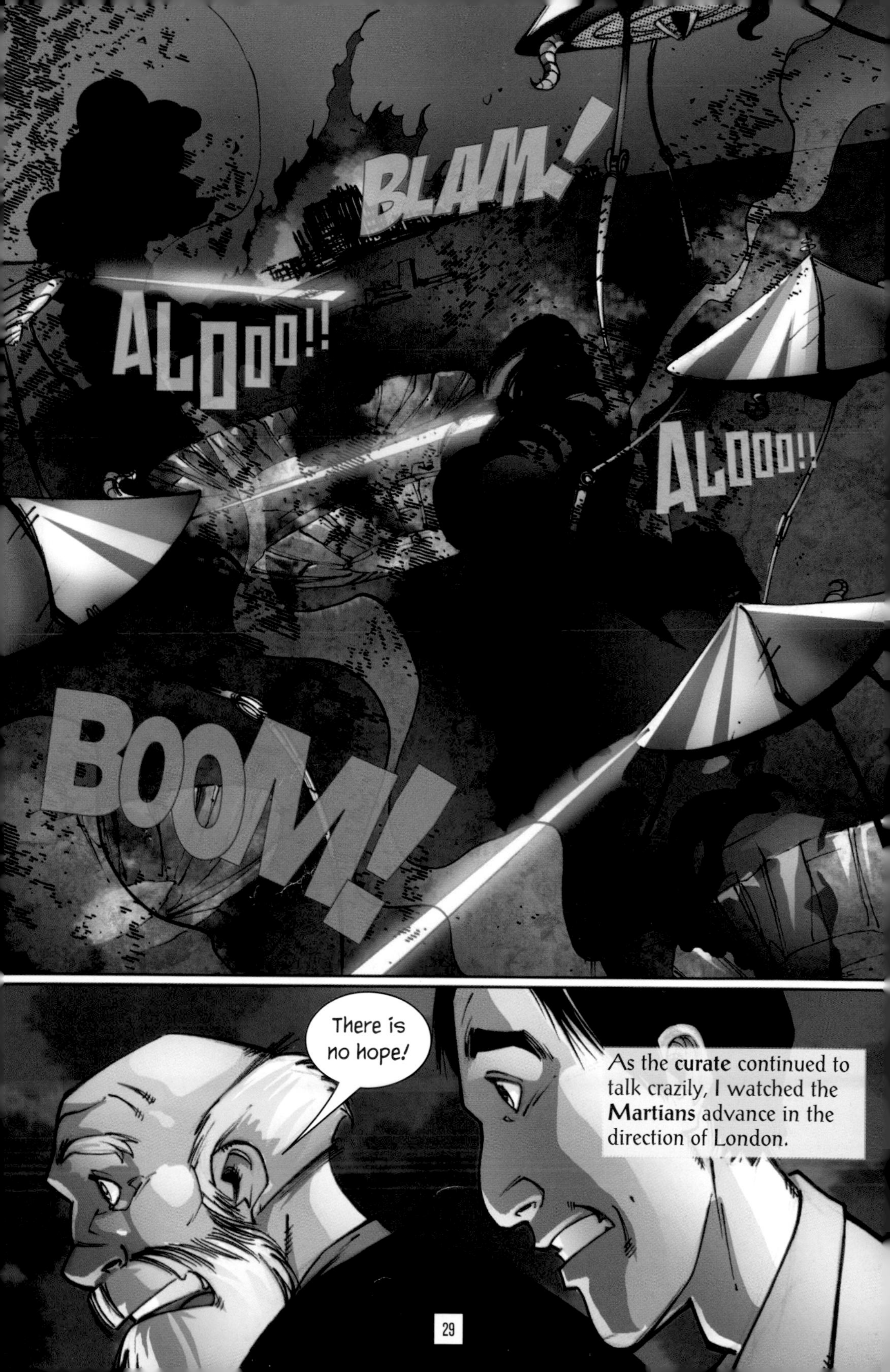
BLAM!
ALOOO!!
ALOOO!!
BOOM!
There is no hope!
As the **curate** continued to talk crazily, I watched the **Martians** advance in the direction of London.

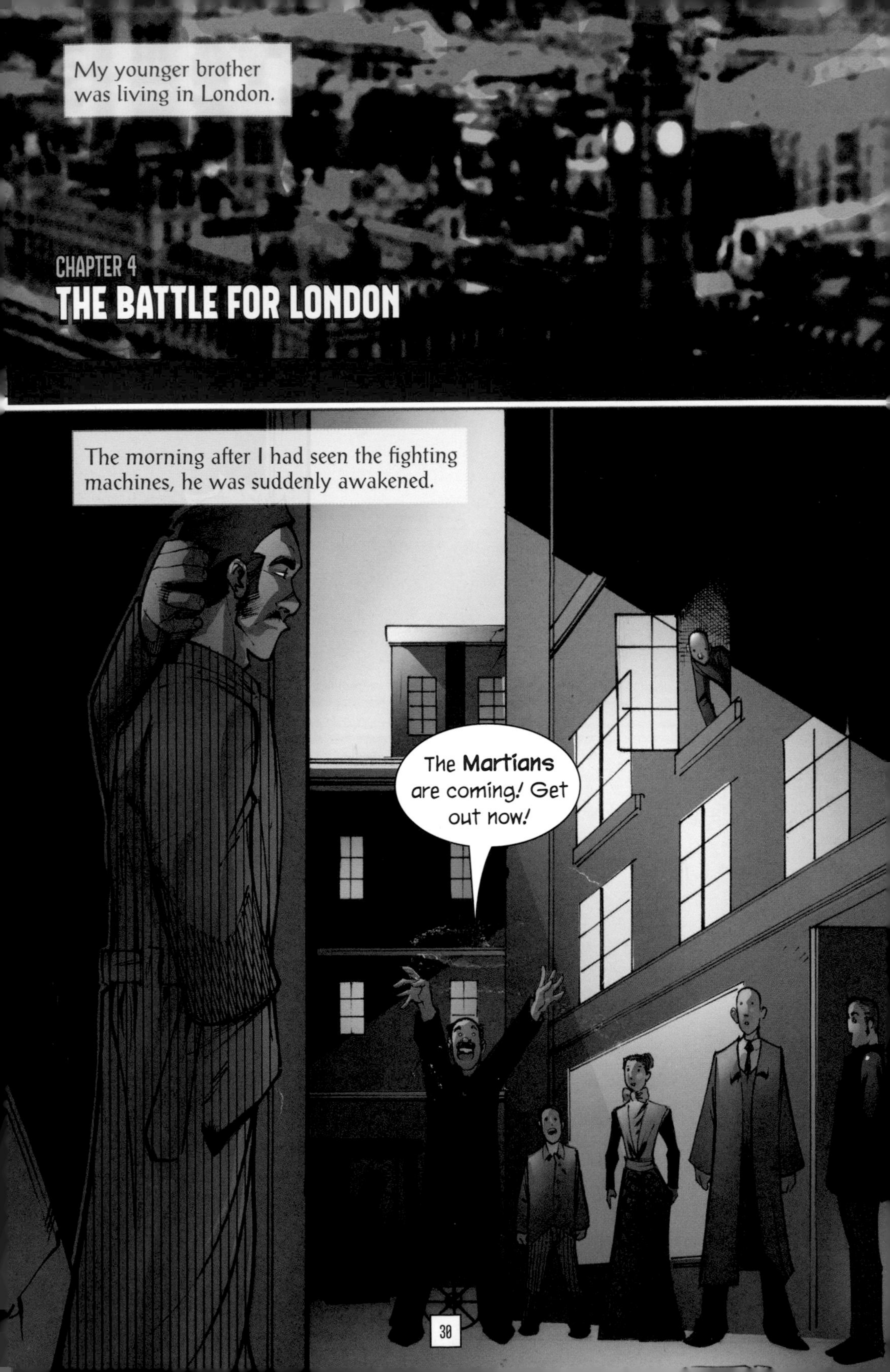
My younger brother was living in London.
CHAPTER 4
THE BATTLE FOR LONDON
The morning after I had seen the fighting machines, he was suddenly awakened.
The Martians are coming! Get out now!

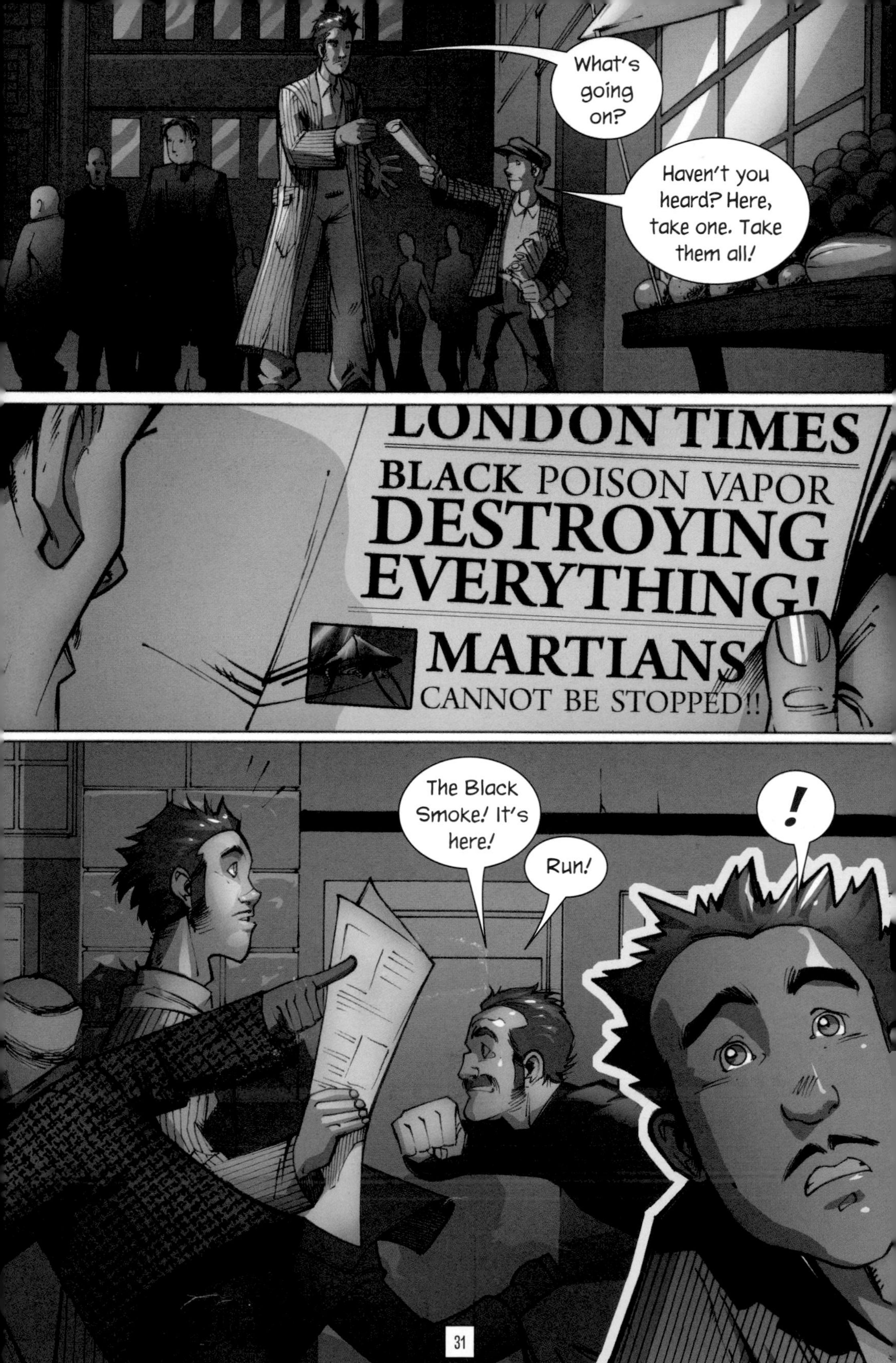
What's going on?
Haven't you heard? Here, take one. Take them all!
LONDON TIMES
BLACK POISON VAPOR
DESTROYING EVERYTHING!
MARTIANS
CANNOT BE STOPPED!!
The Black Smoke! It's here!
Run!
!

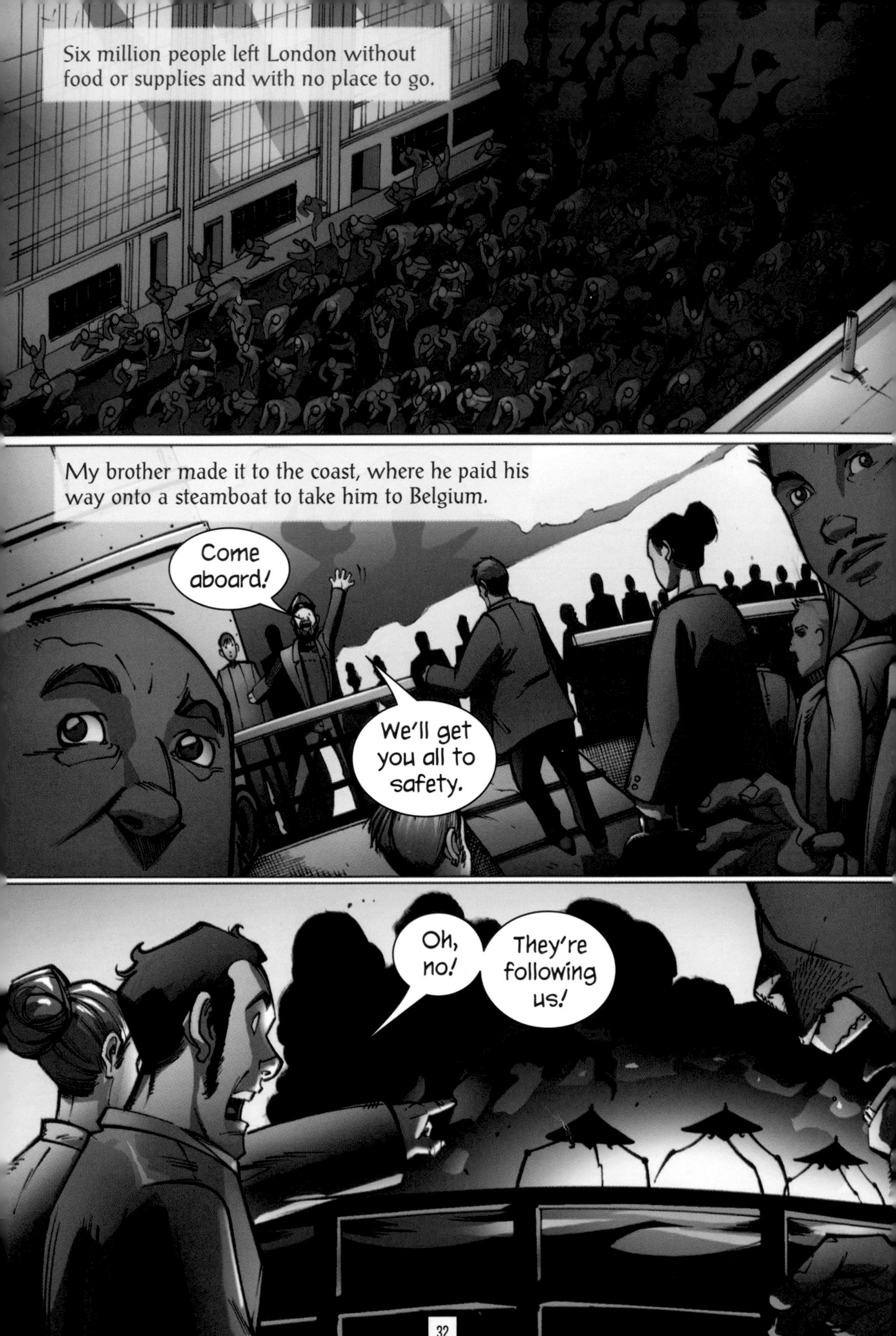
Six million people left London without food or supplies and with no place to go.
My brother made it to the coast, where he paid his way onto a steamboat to take him to Belgium.
Come aboard!
We'll get you all to safety.
Oh, no!
They're following us!

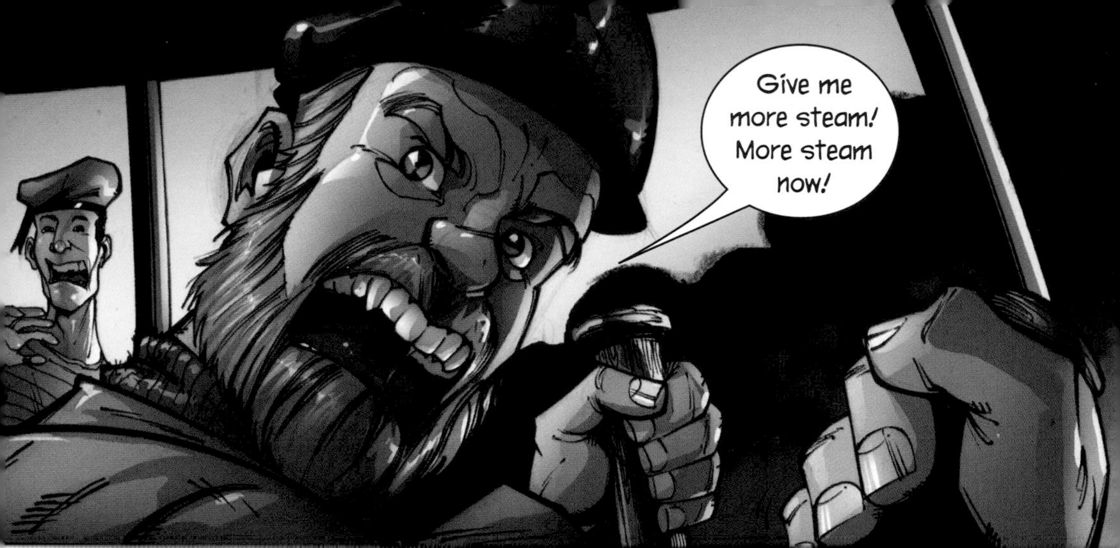
Give me more steam! More steam now!

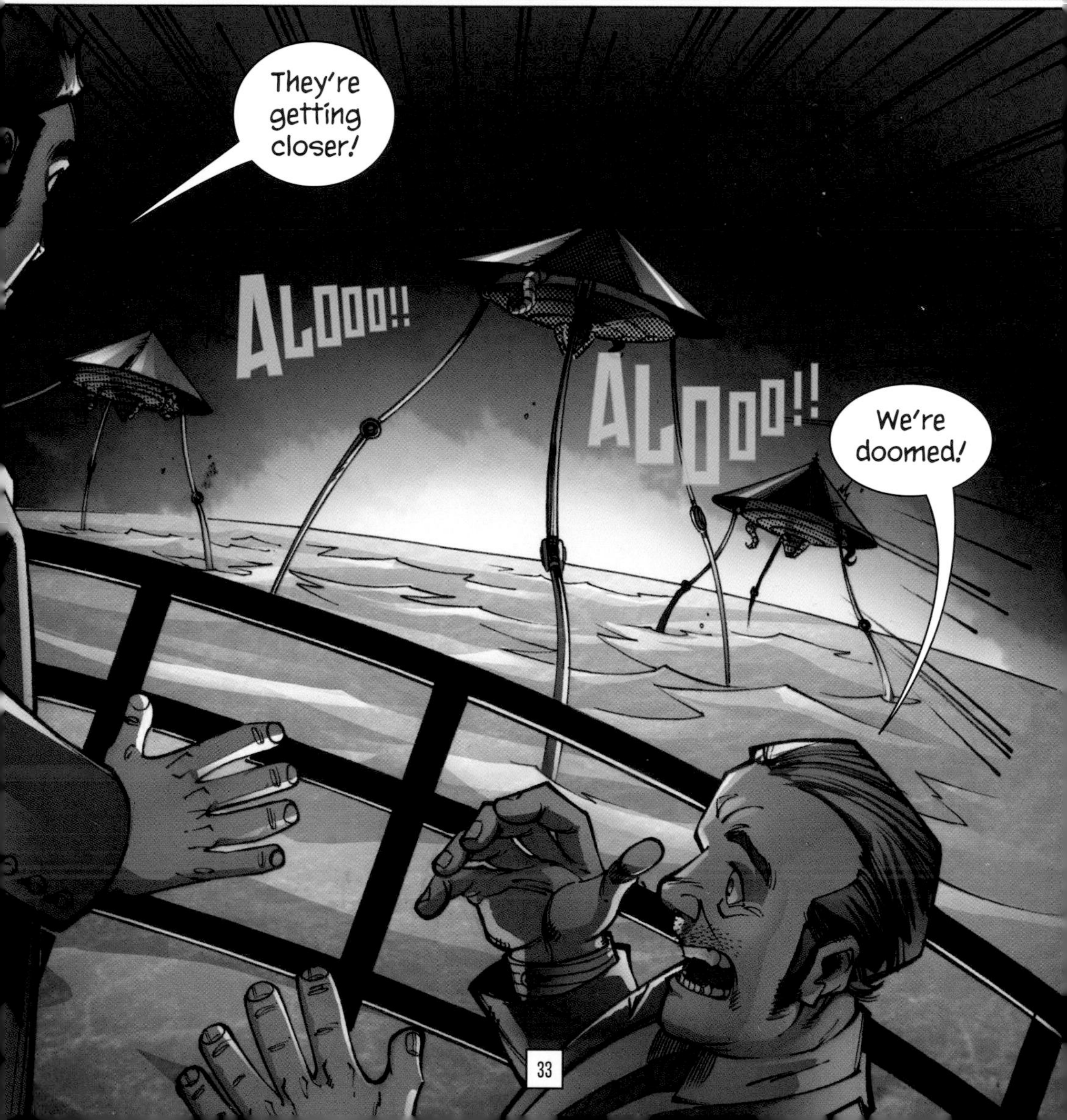
They're getting closer!
ALOOO!!
ALOOO!!
We're doomed!

Then suddenly . . .

Look!

It was the fighting ship, *Thunder Child*, steaming to the rescue.

BLAM!

BLAM!

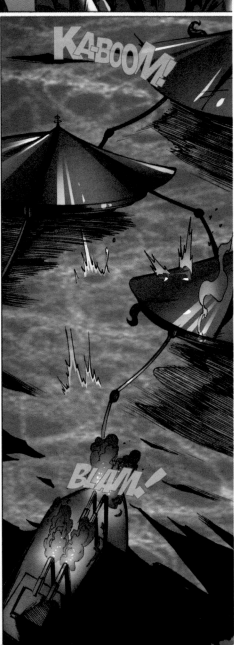

KA-BOOM!

BLAM!

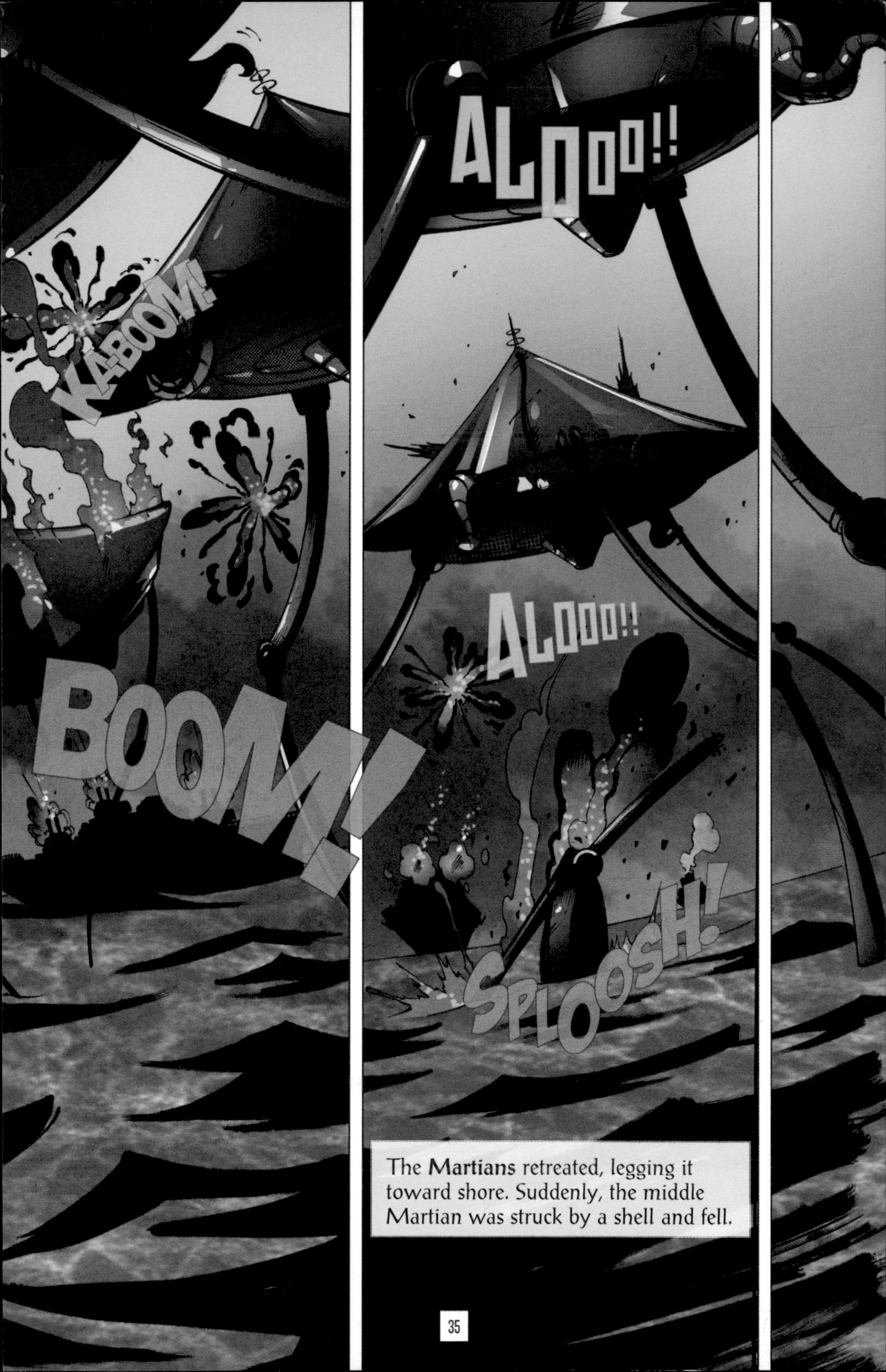
KA-BOOM!
BOOM!
ALOOO!!
ALOOO!!
SPLOOSH!
The Martians retreated, legging it toward shore. Suddenly, the middle Martian was struck by a shell and fell.

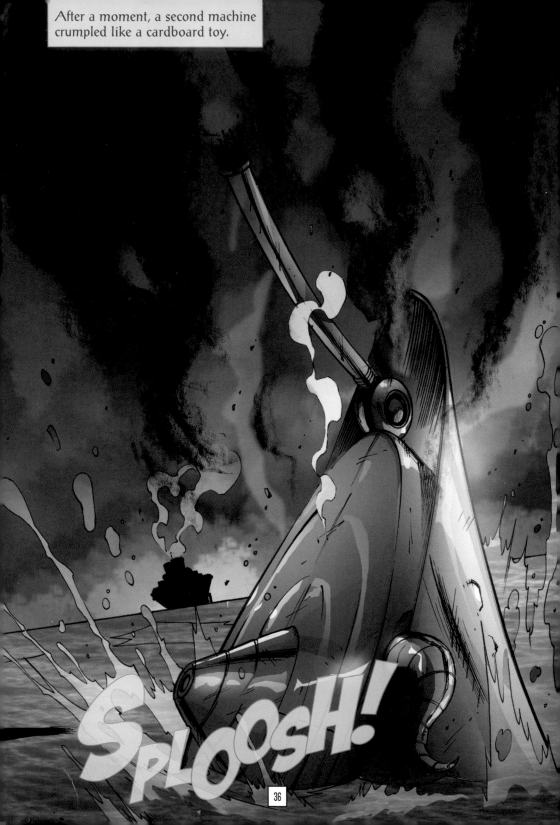

After a moment, a second machine crumpled like a cardboard toy.

SPLOOSH!

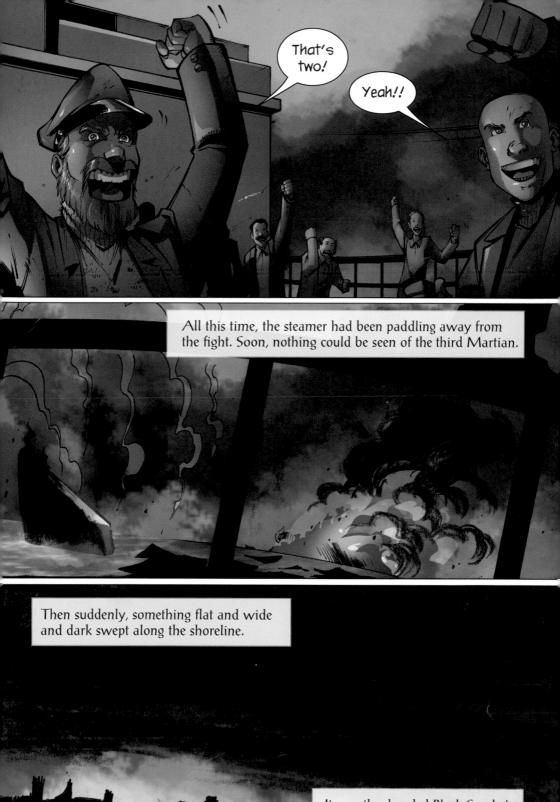

That's two!

Yeah!!

All this time, the steamer had been paddling away from the fight. Soon, nothing could be seen of the third Martian.

Then suddenly, something flat and wide and dark swept along the shoreline.

It was the dreaded Black Smoke!

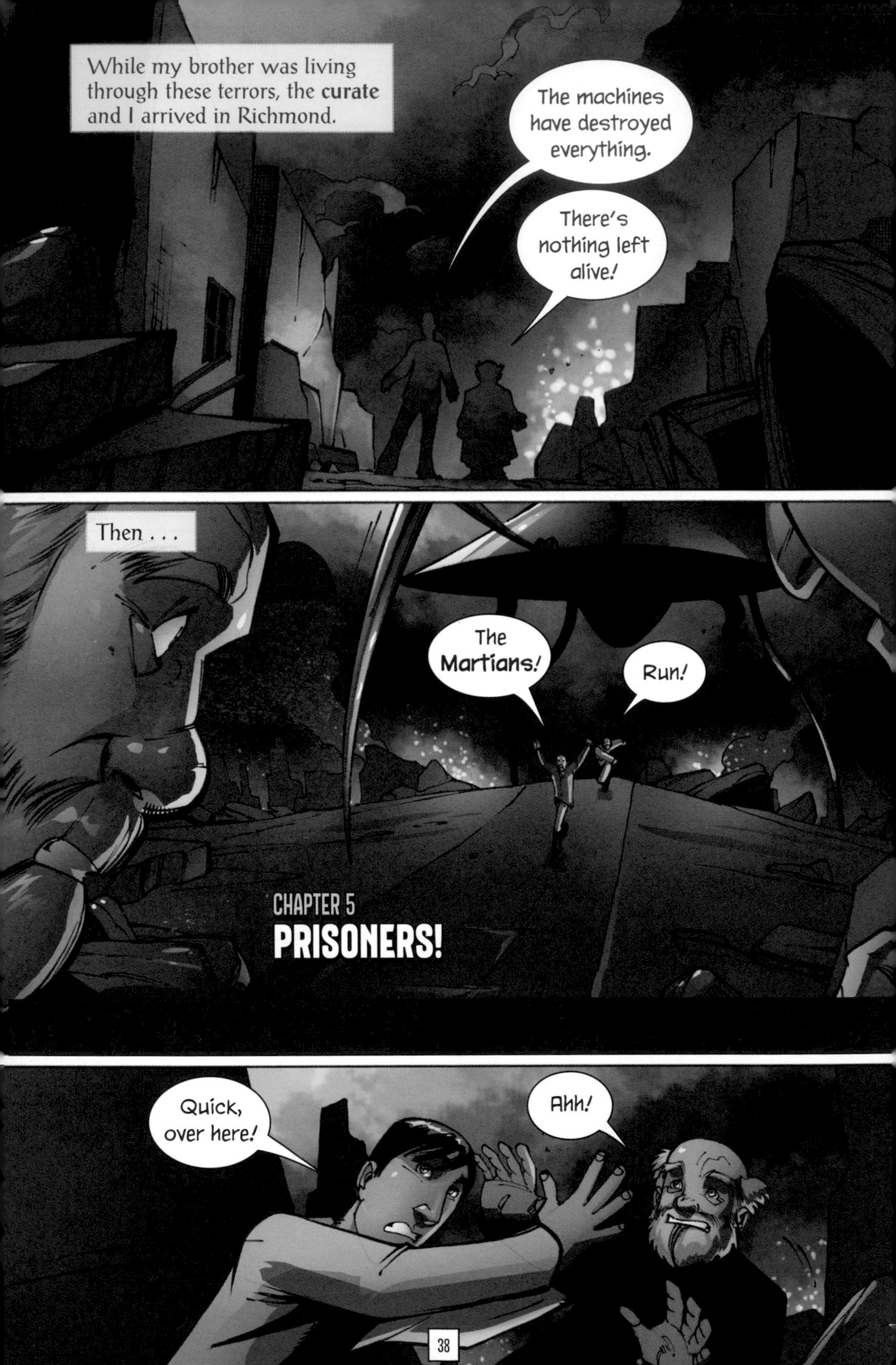
While my brother was living through these terrors, the **curate** and I arrived in Richmond.
The machines have destroyed everything.
There's nothing left alive!
Then . . .
The **Martians**!
Run!
CHAPTER 5
PRISONERS!
Quick, over here!
Ahh!

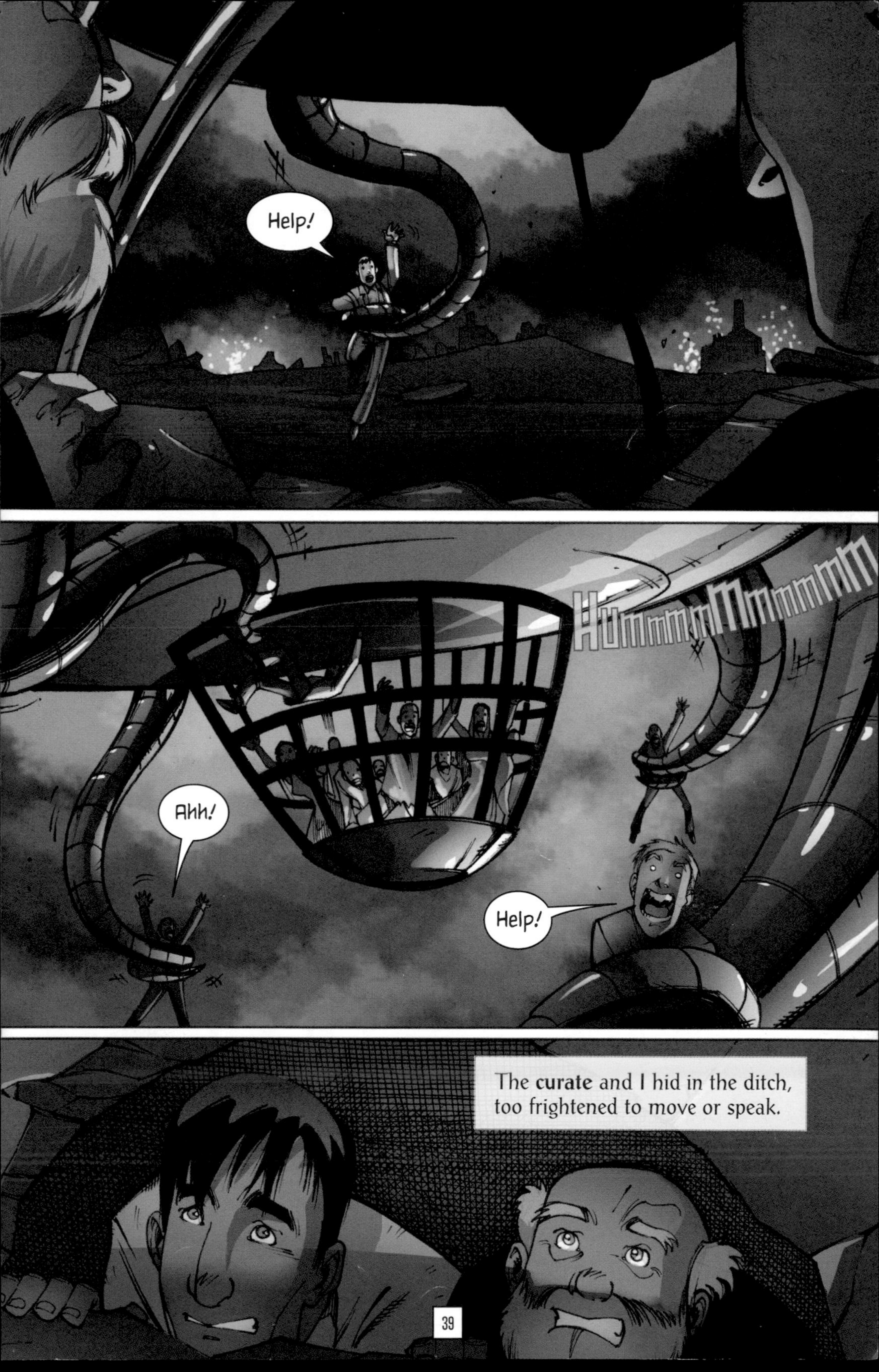
Help!
HUmmmmMmmmmM
Ahh!
Help!
The curate and I hid in the ditch, too frightened to move or speak.

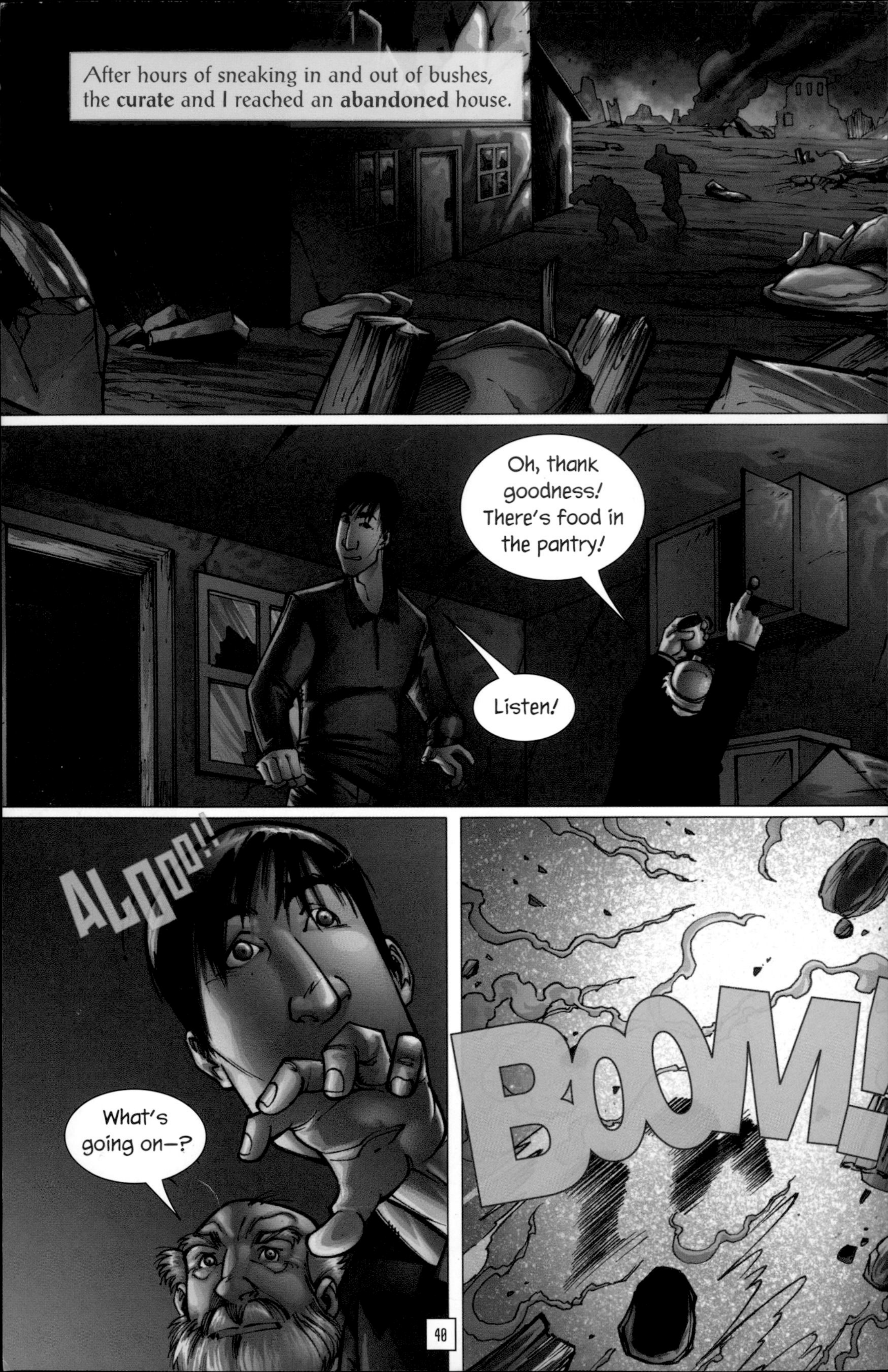
After hours of sneaking in and out of bushes, the **curate** and I reached an **abandoned** house.
Oh, thank goodness! There's food in the pantry!
Listen!
ALOOO!!
What's going on–?
BOOM!

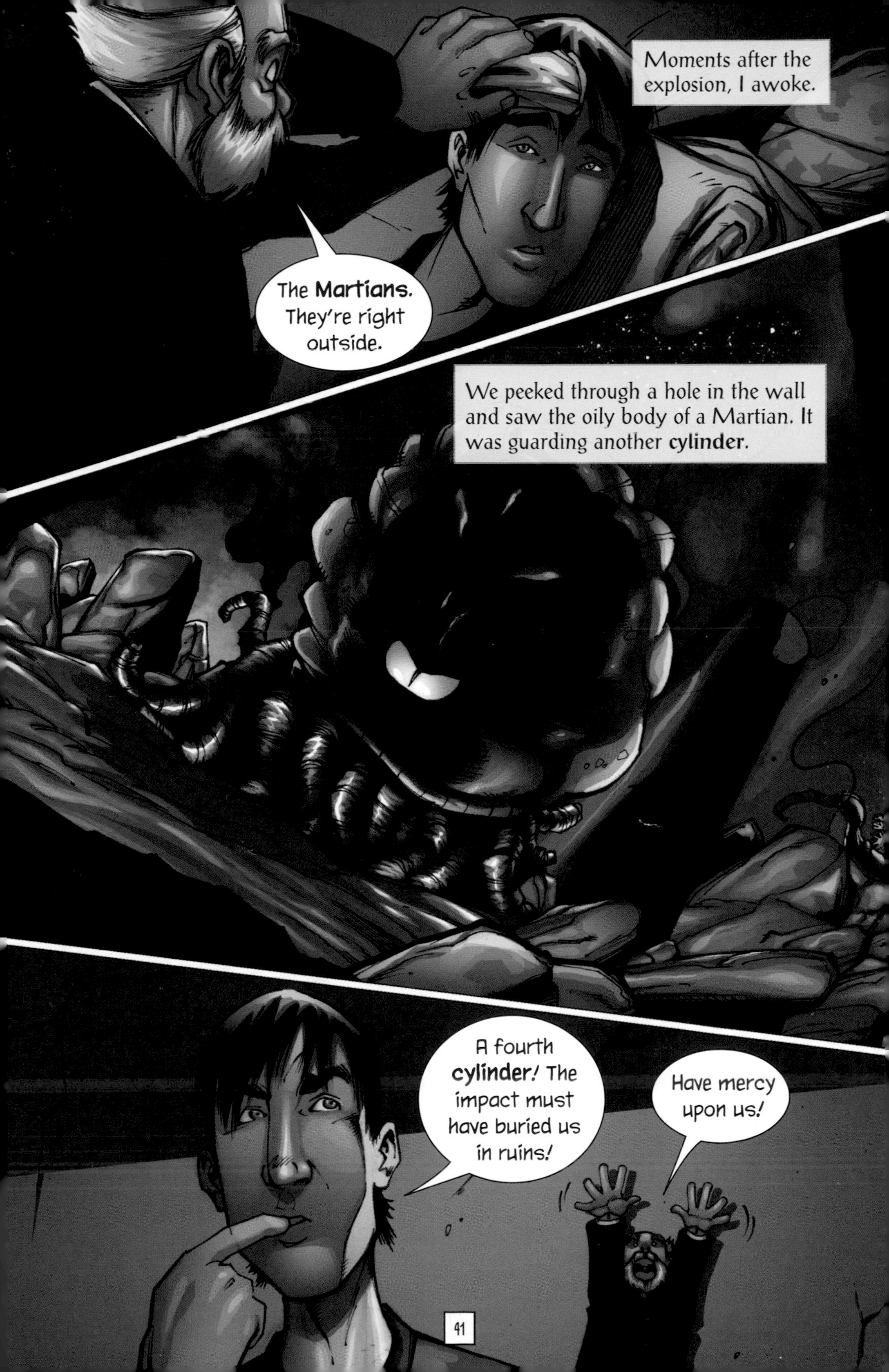
Moments after the explosion, I awoke.
The Martians. They're right outside.
We peeked through a hole in the wall and saw the oily body of a Martian. It was guarding another cylinder.
A fourth cylinder! The impact must have buried us in ruins!
Have mercy upon us!

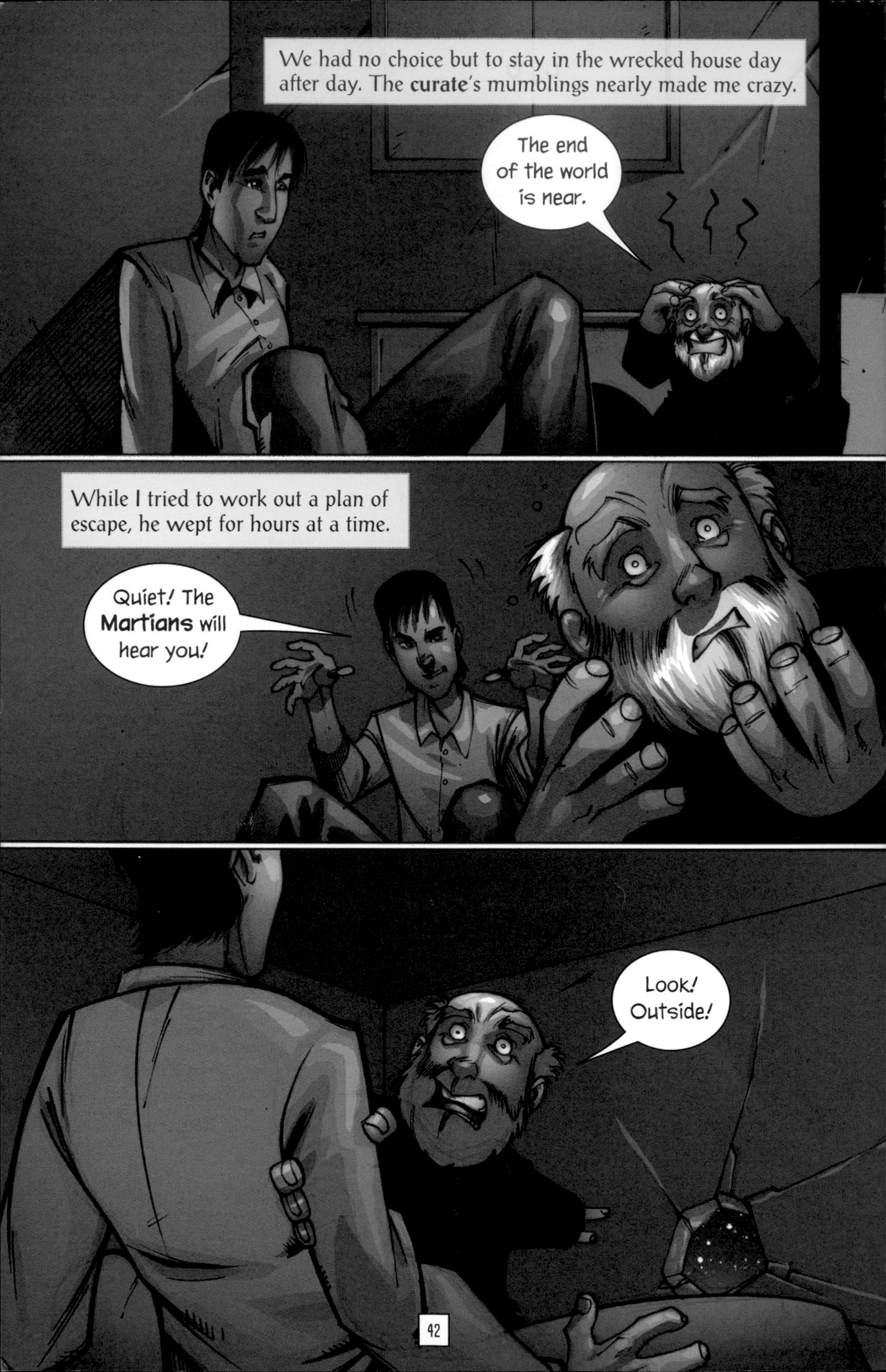
We had no choice but to stay in the wrecked house day after day. The **curate**'s mumblings nearly made me crazy.
The end of the world is near.
While I tried to work out a plan of escape, he wept for hours at a time.
Quiet! The **Martians** will hear you!
Look! Outside!

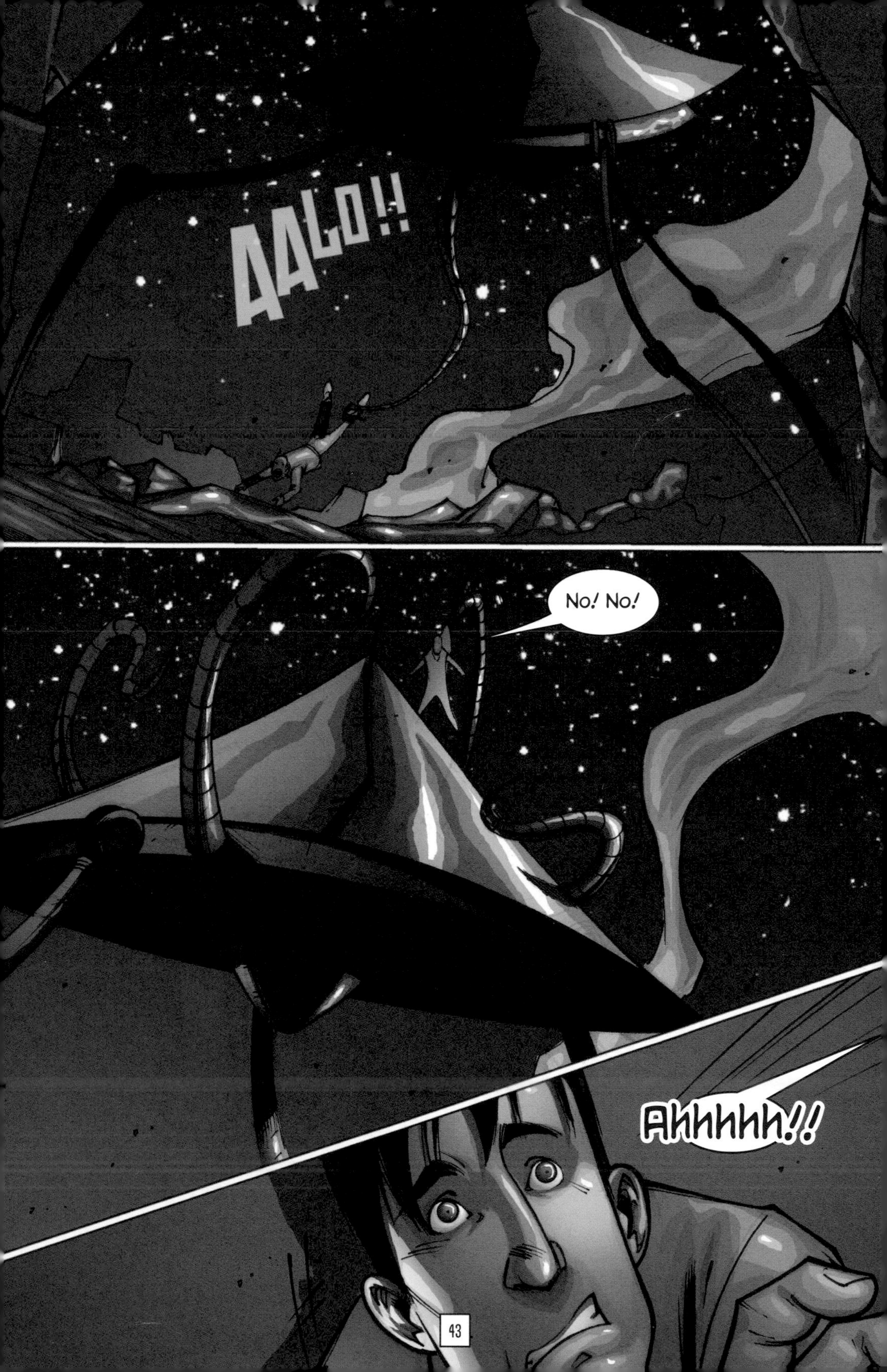
AALO!!
No! No!
Ahhhhh!!

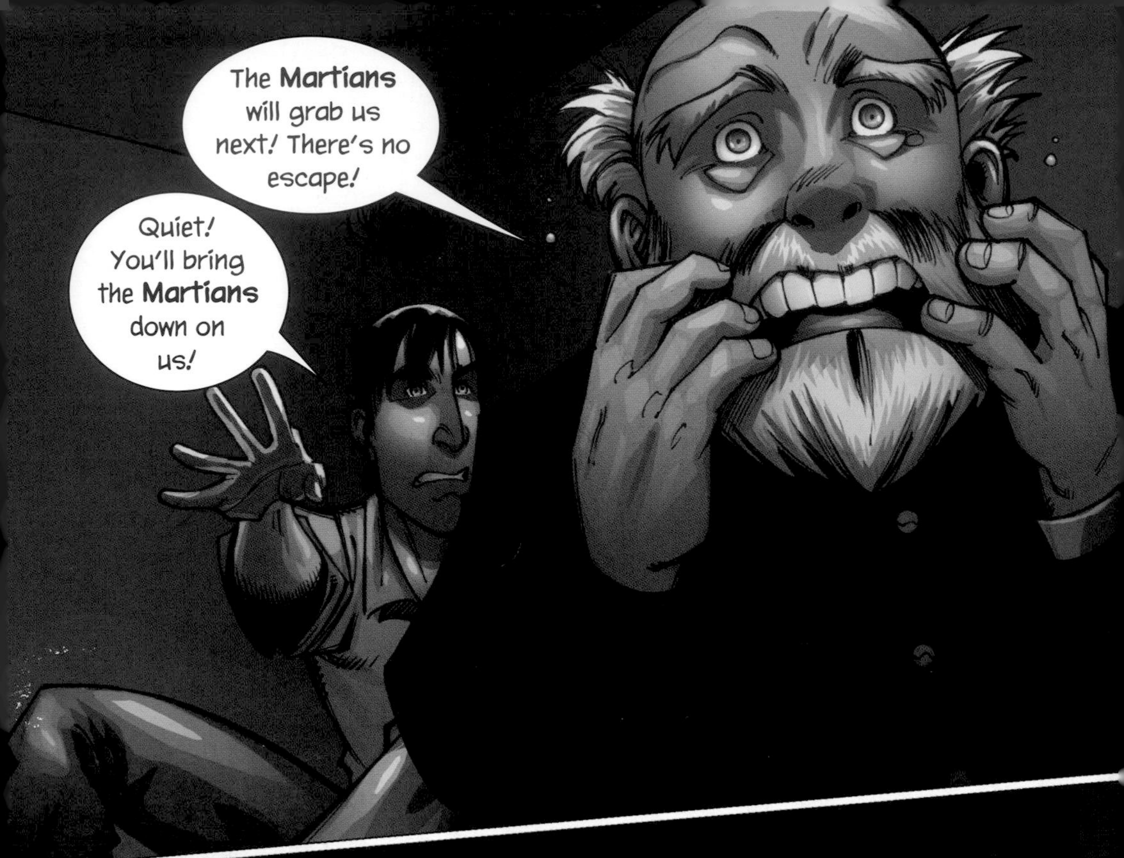
The **Martians** will grab us next! There's no escape!
Quiet! You'll bring the **Martians** down on us!

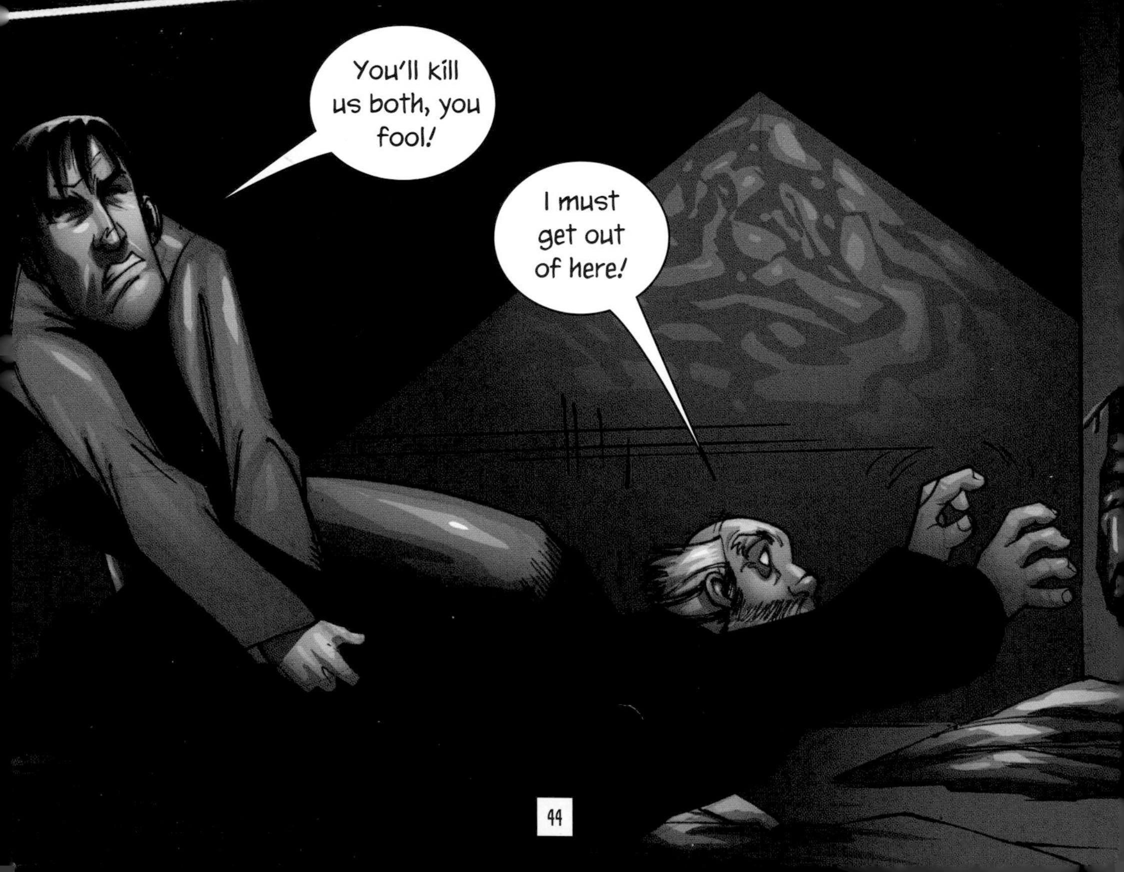
You'll kill us both, you fool!
I must get out of here!

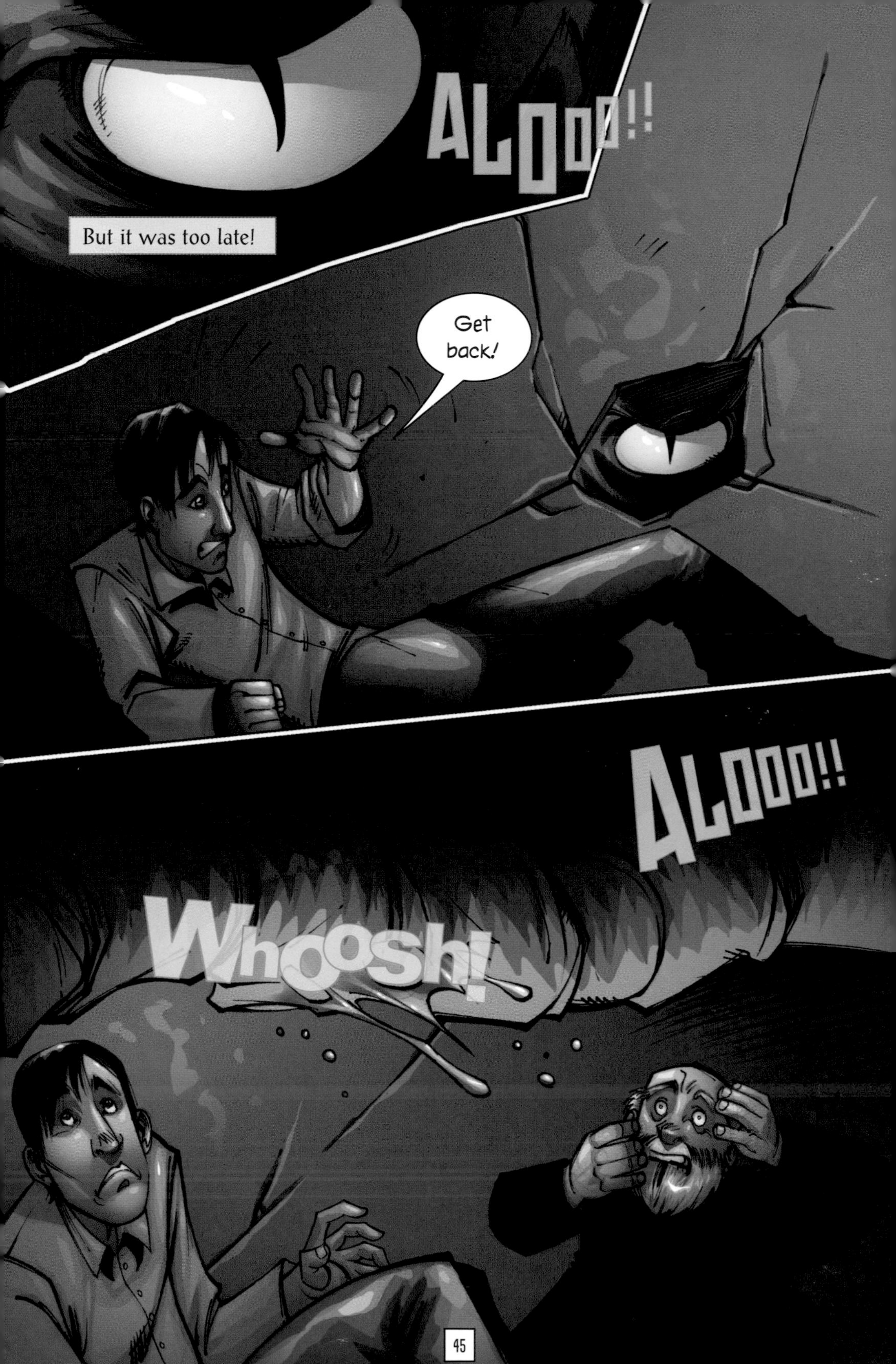
ALOOO!!
But it was too late!
Get back!
ALOOO!!
Whoosh!

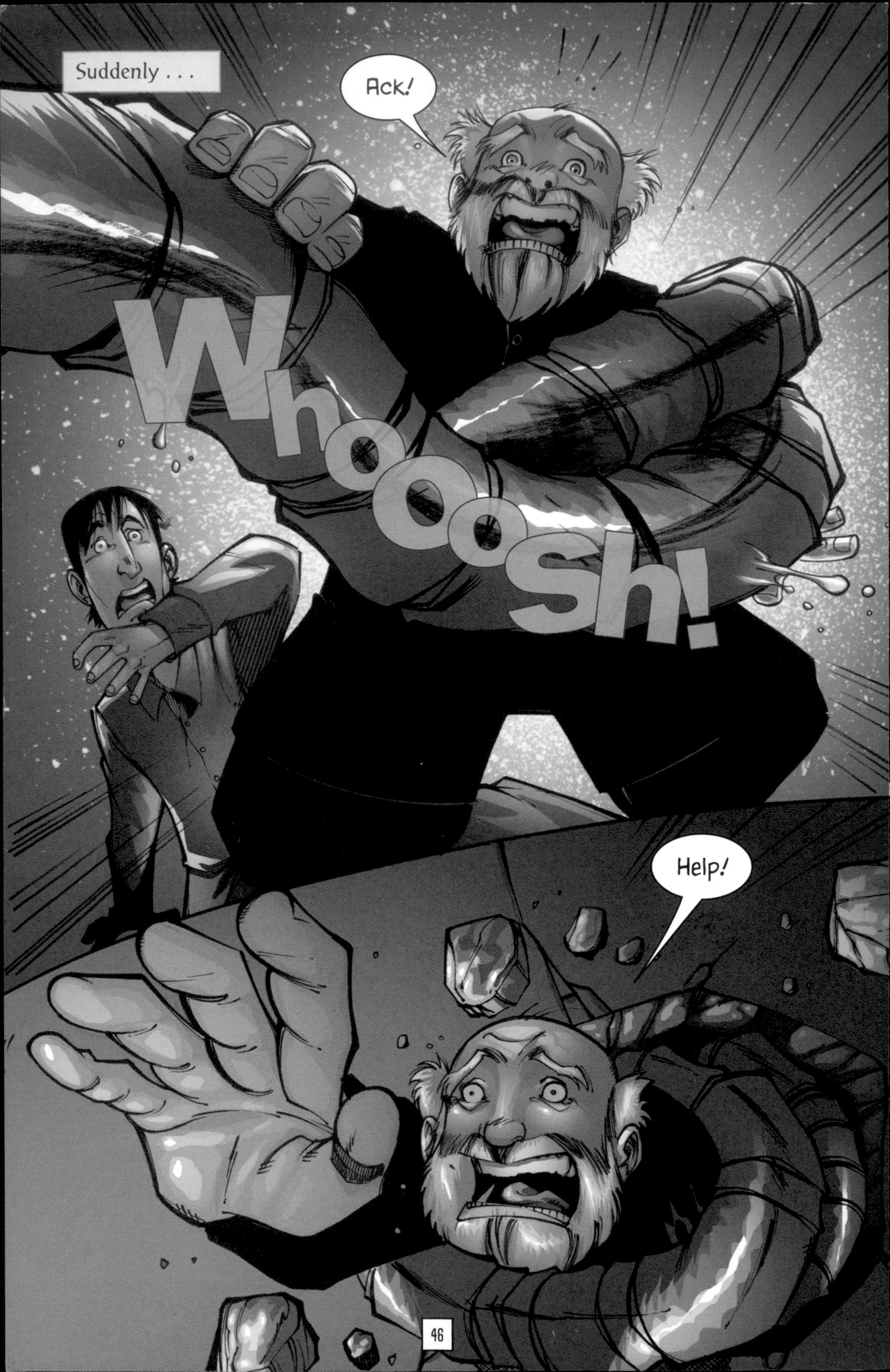
Suddenly . . .
Ack!
Whooosh!
Help!

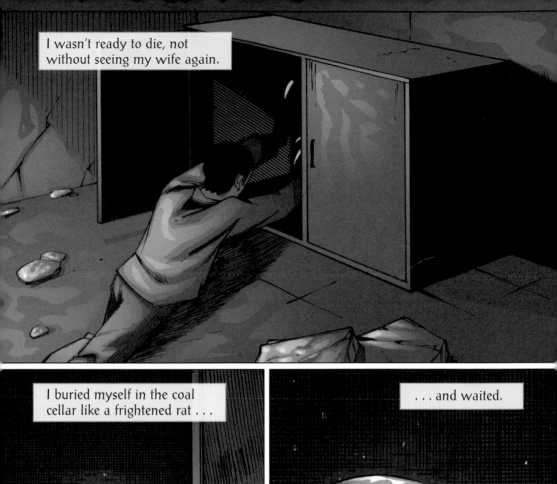

I wasn't ready to die, not without seeing my wife again.

I buried myself in the coal cellar like a frightened rat . . .

. . . and waited.

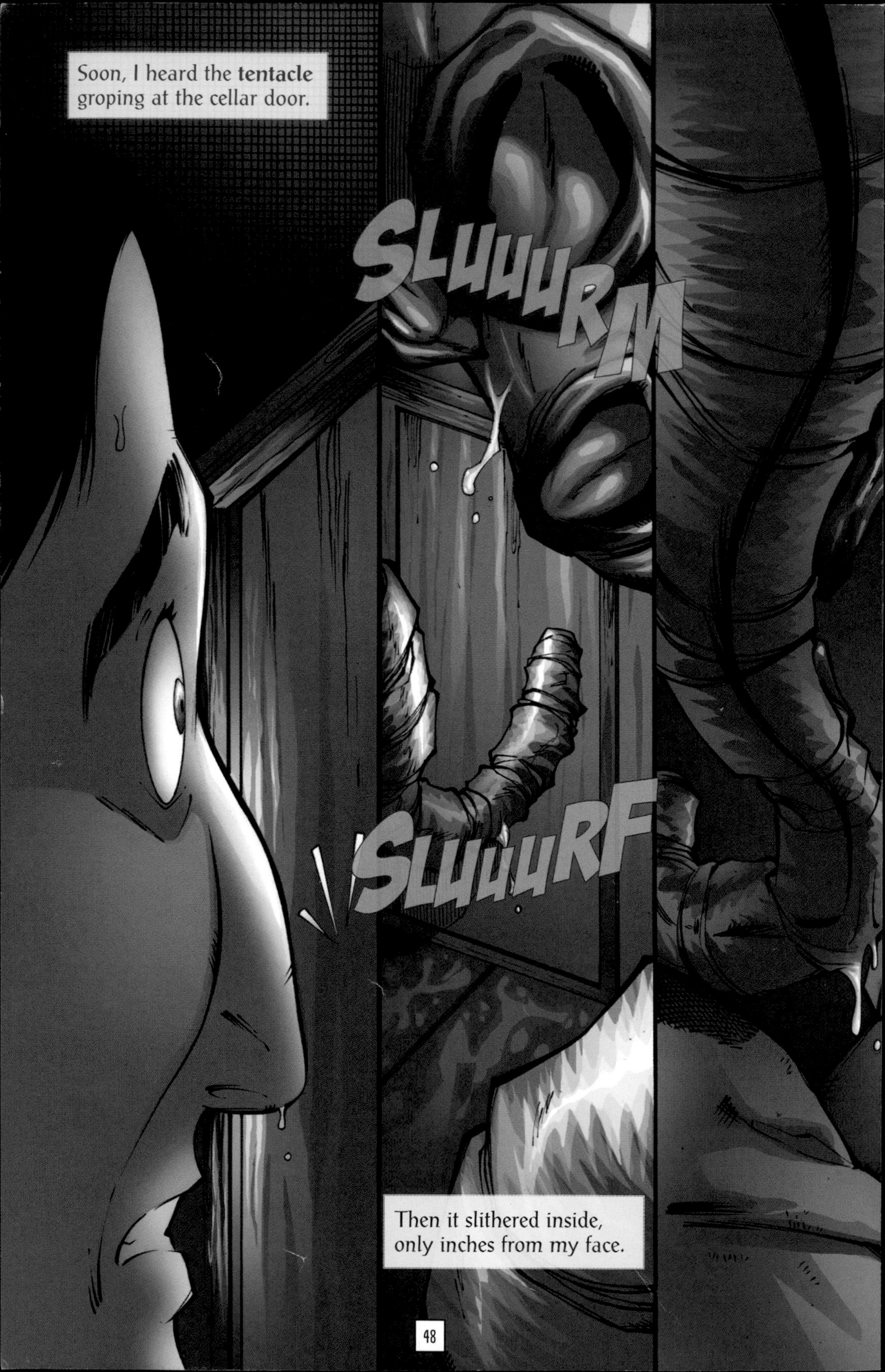

Soon, I heard the **tentacle** groping at the cellar door.
SLUUURM
SLUUURF
Then it slithered inside, only inches from my face.

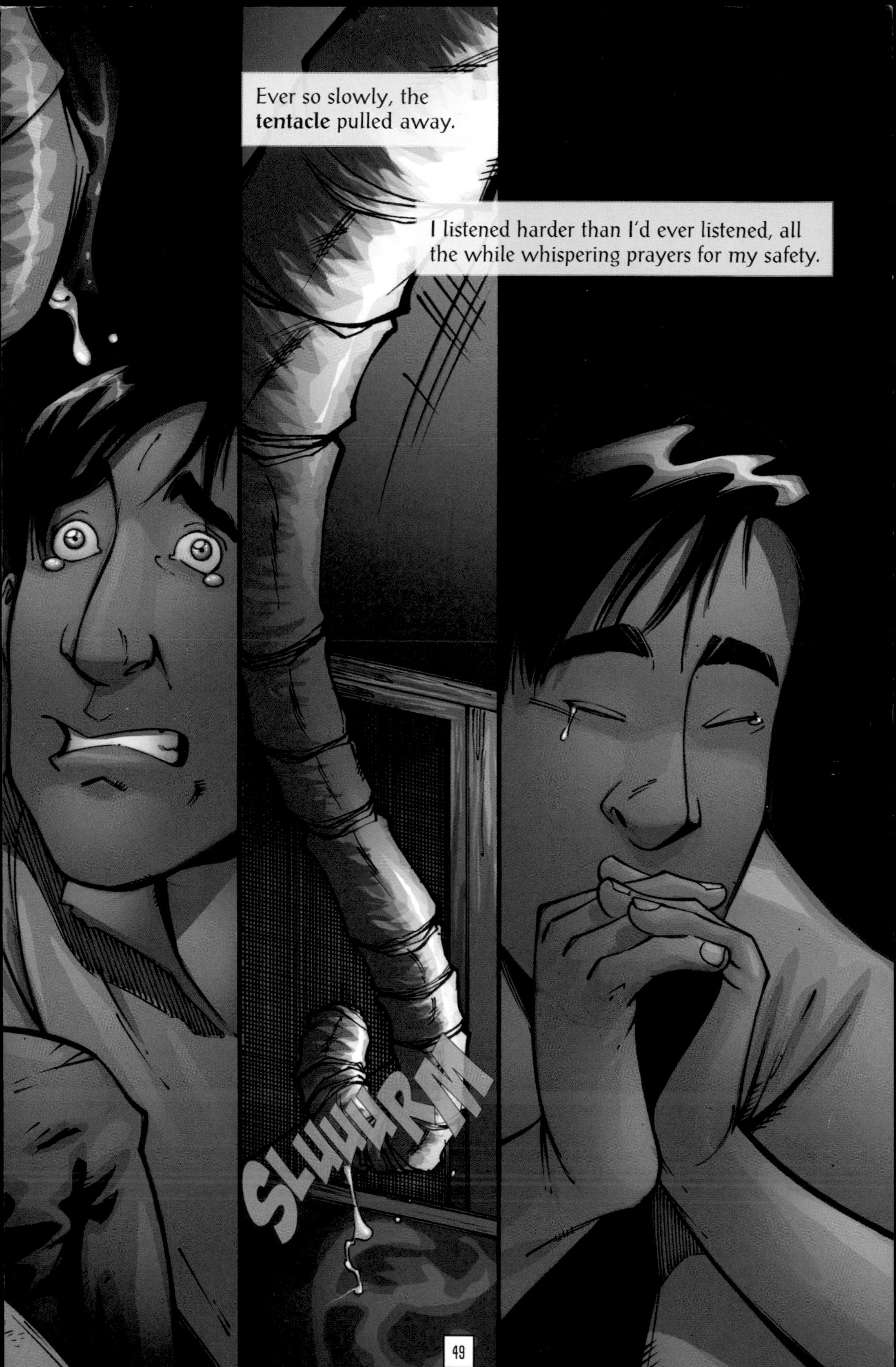
Ever so slowly, the **tentacle** pulled away.
I listened harder than I'd ever listened, all the while whispering prayers for my safety.
SLUURM

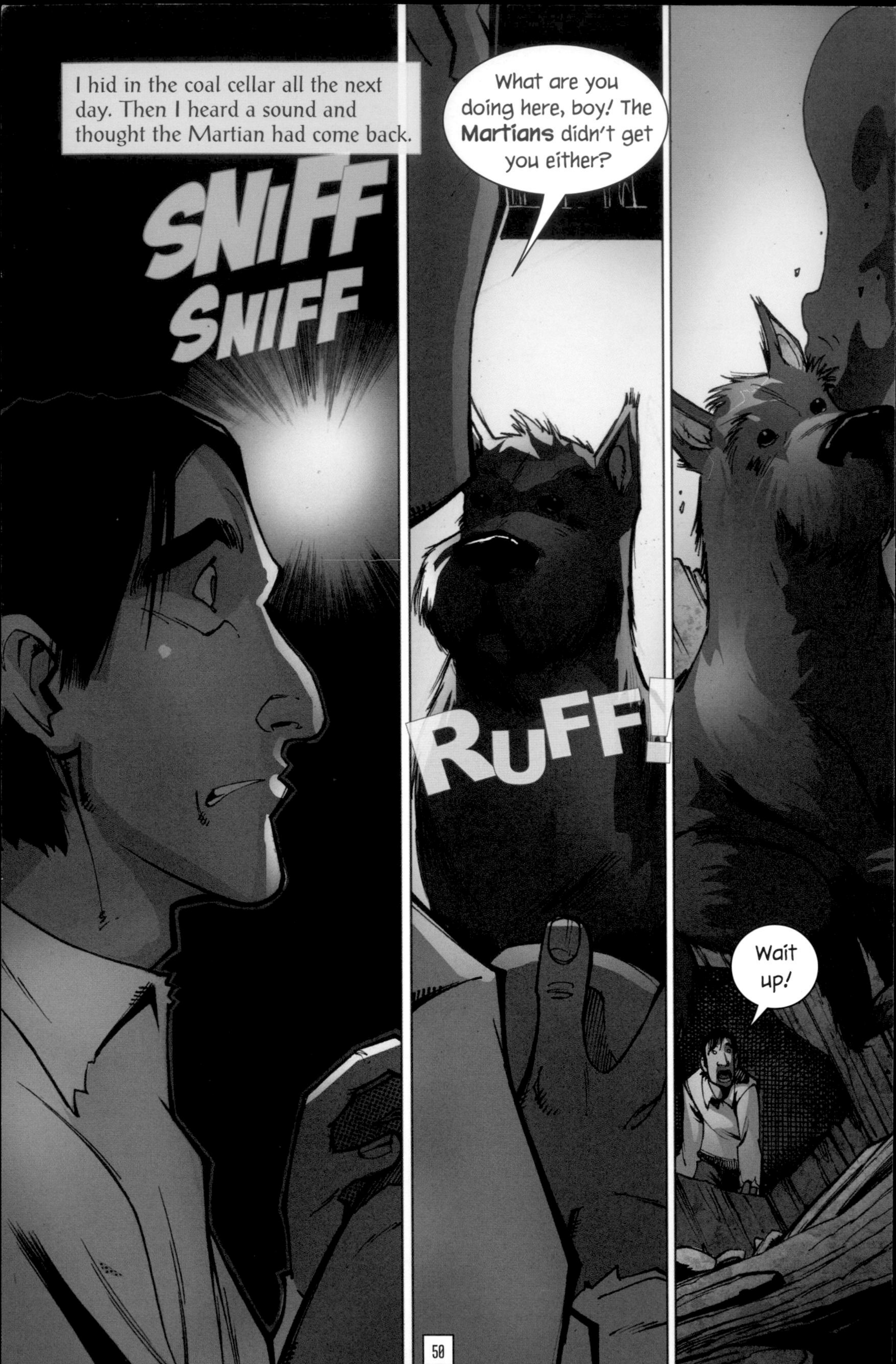
I hid in the coal cellar all the next day. Then I heard a sound and thought the Martian had come back.
SNIFF SNIFF
What are you doing here, boy! The Martians didn't get you either?
RUFF!
Wait up!

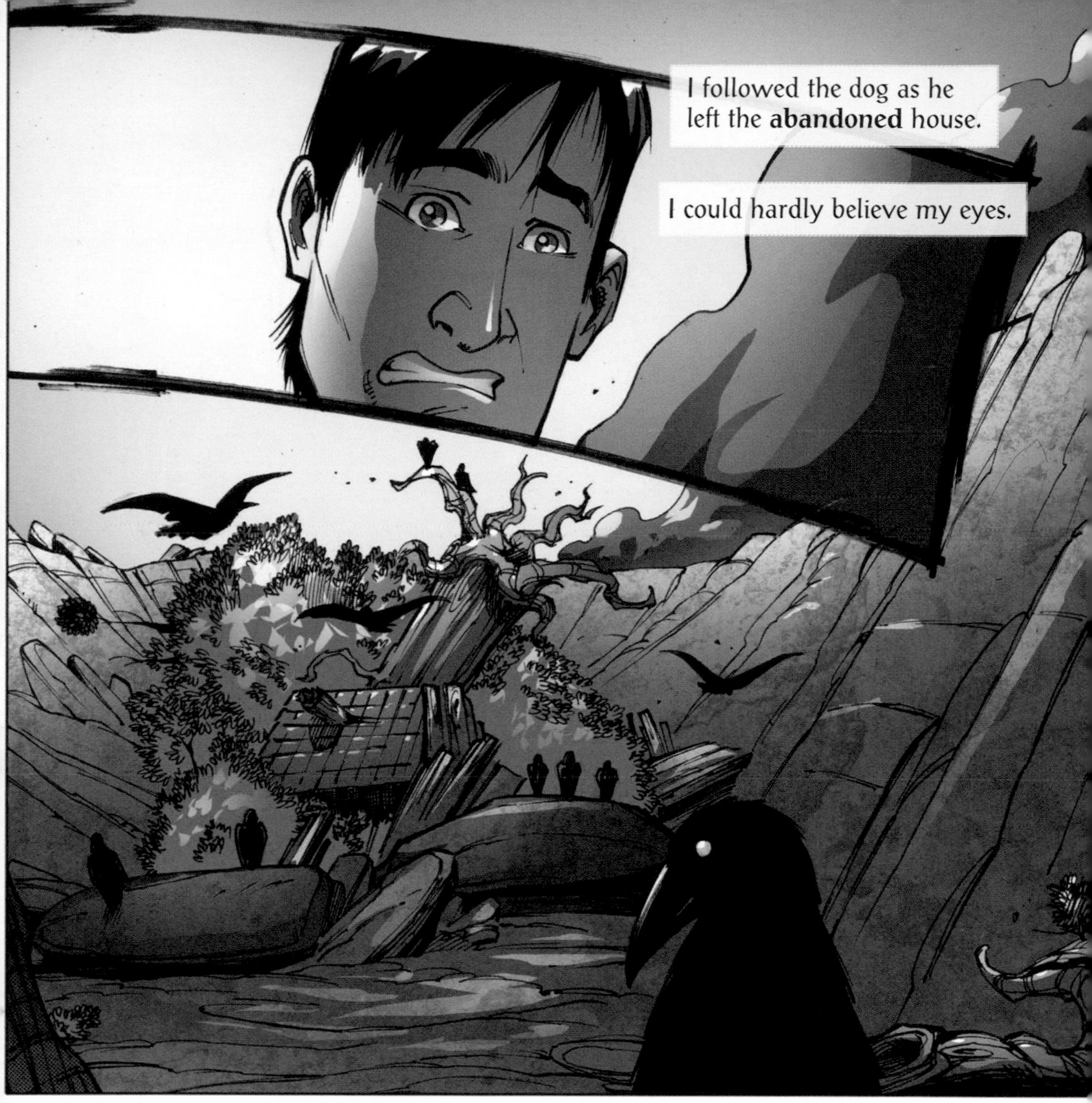
I followed the dog as he left the **abandoned** house.
I could hardly believe my eyes.

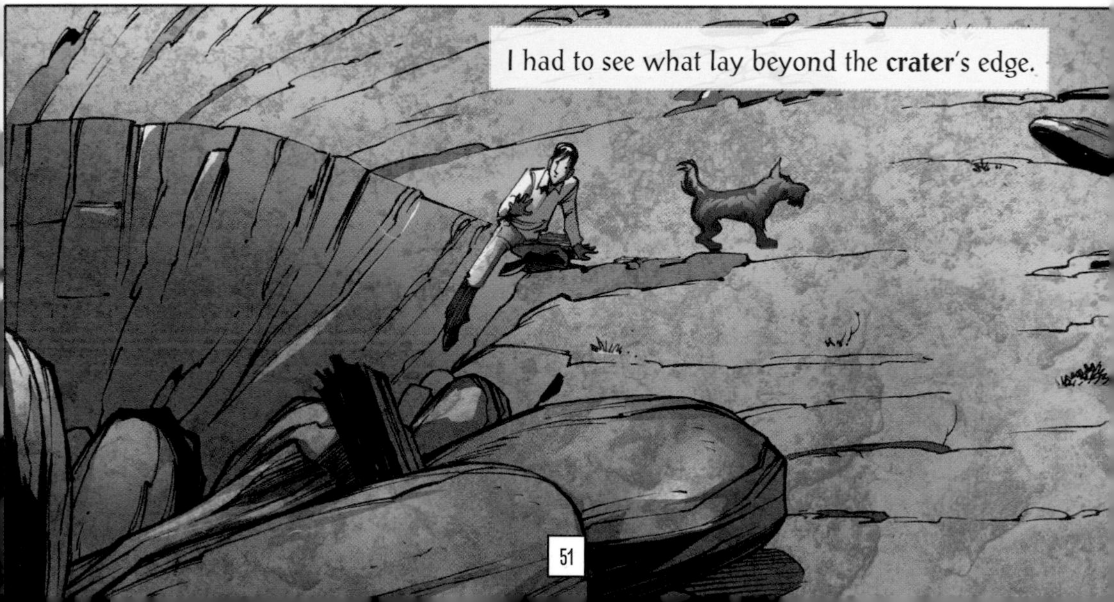
I had to see what lay beyond the **crater**'s edge.

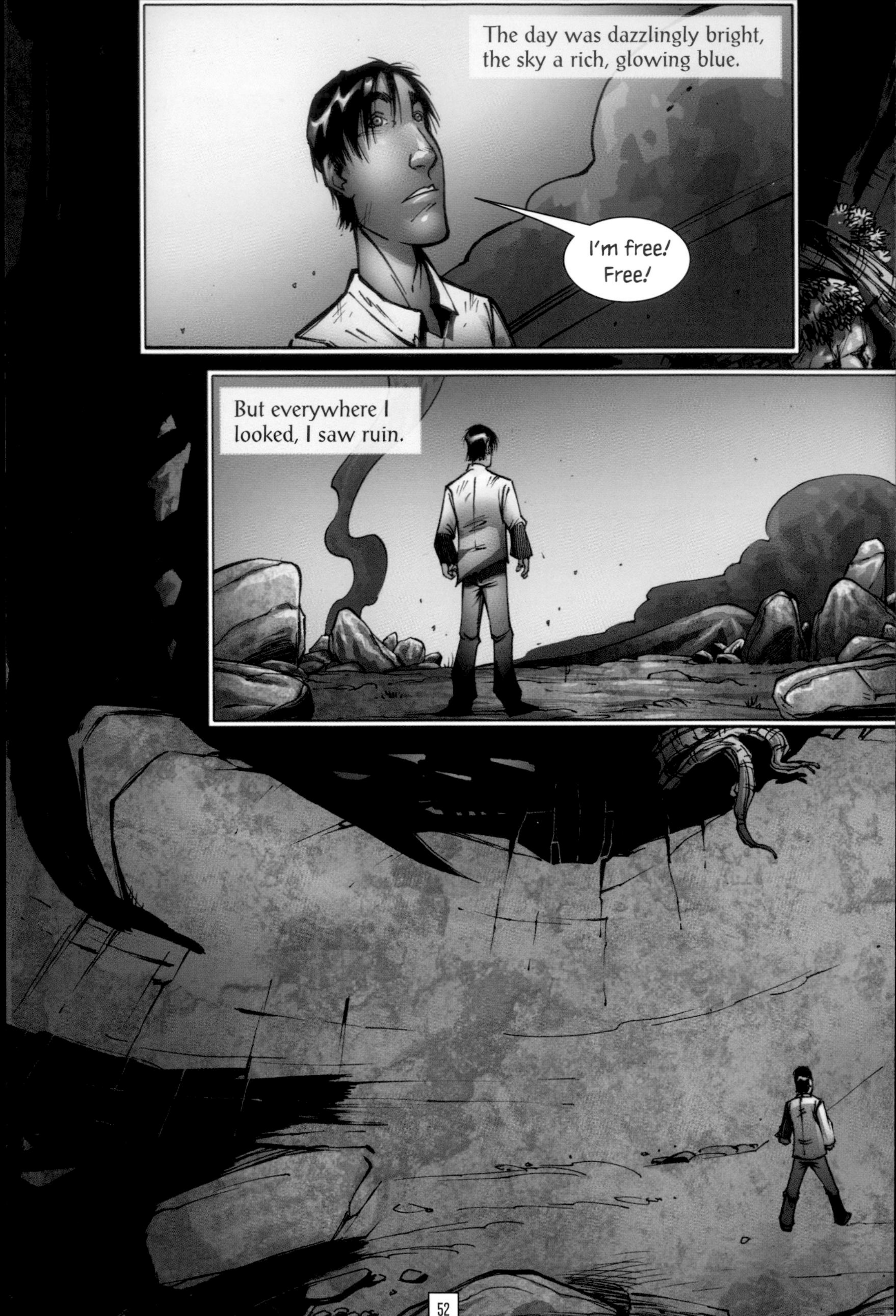
The day was dazzlingly bright, the sky a rich, glowing blue.
I'm free! Free!
But everywhere I looked, I saw ruin.

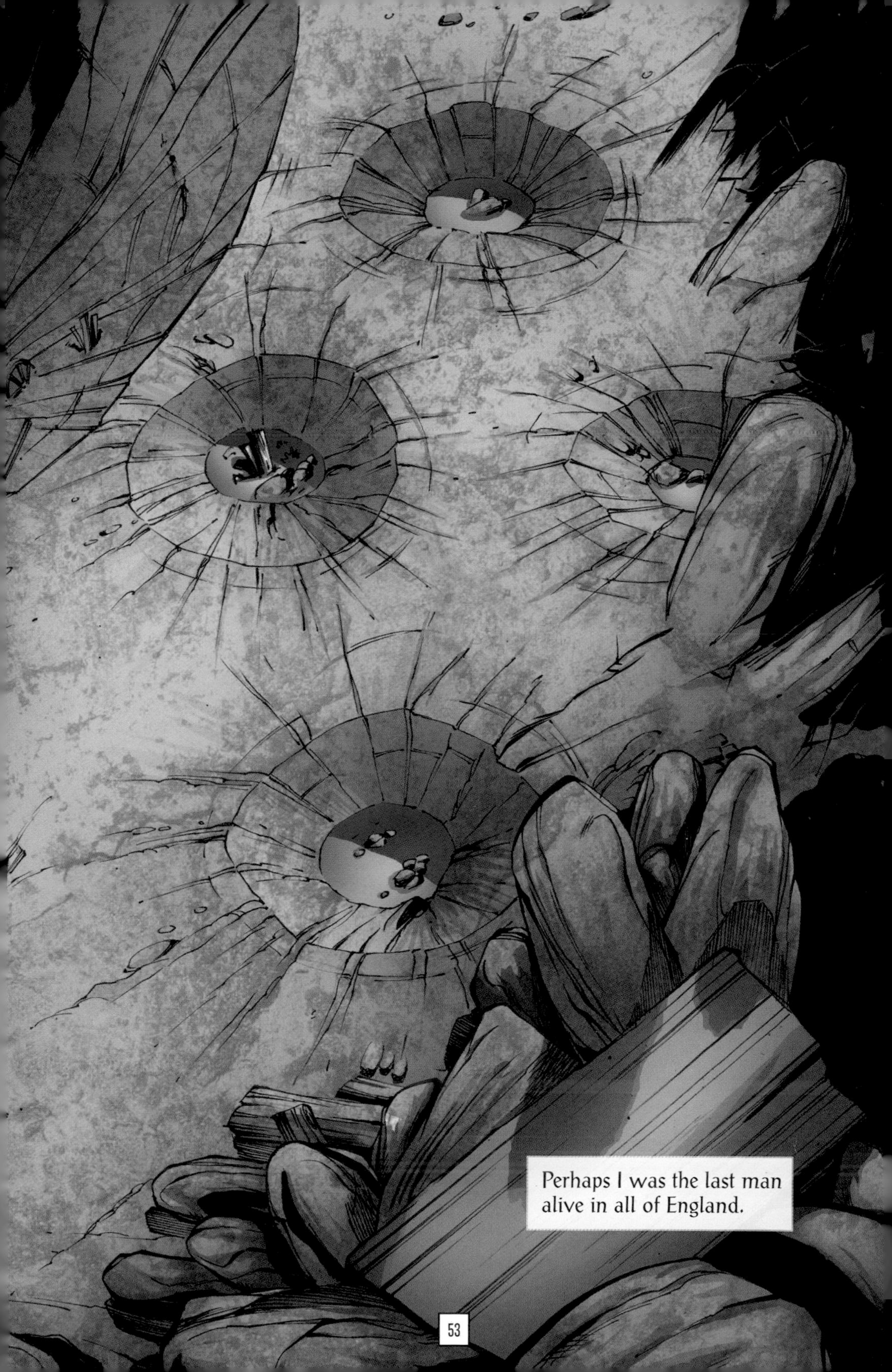
Perhaps I was the last man alive in all of England.

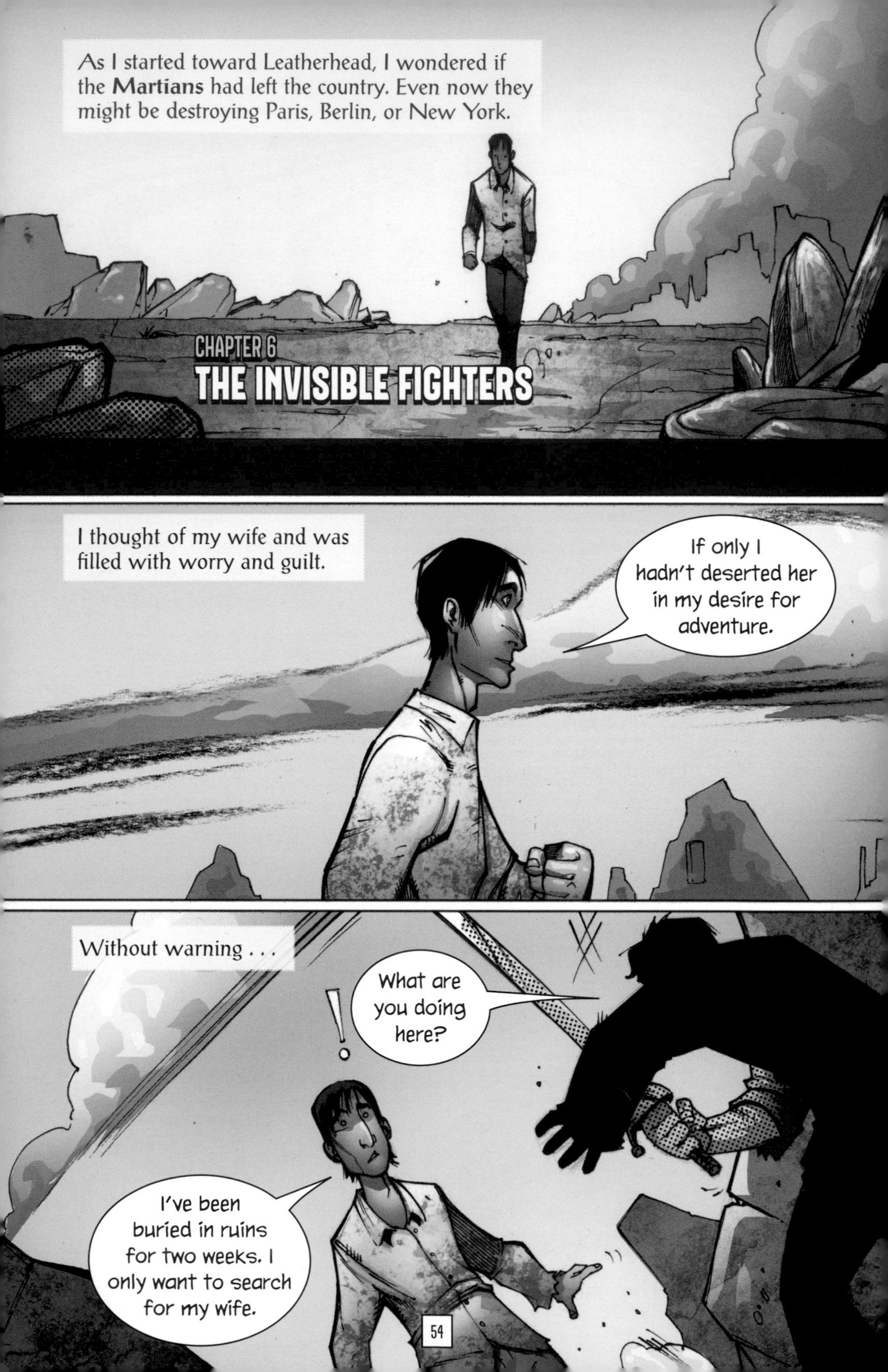
As I started toward Leatherhead, I wondered if the **Martians** had left the country. Even now they might be destroying Paris, Berlin, or New York.
CHAPTER 6
THE INVISIBLE FIGHTERS
I thought of my wife and was filled with worry and guilt.
If only I hadn't deserted her in my desire for adventure.
Without warning . . .
!
What are you doing here?
I've been buried in ruins for two weeks. I only want to search for my wife.

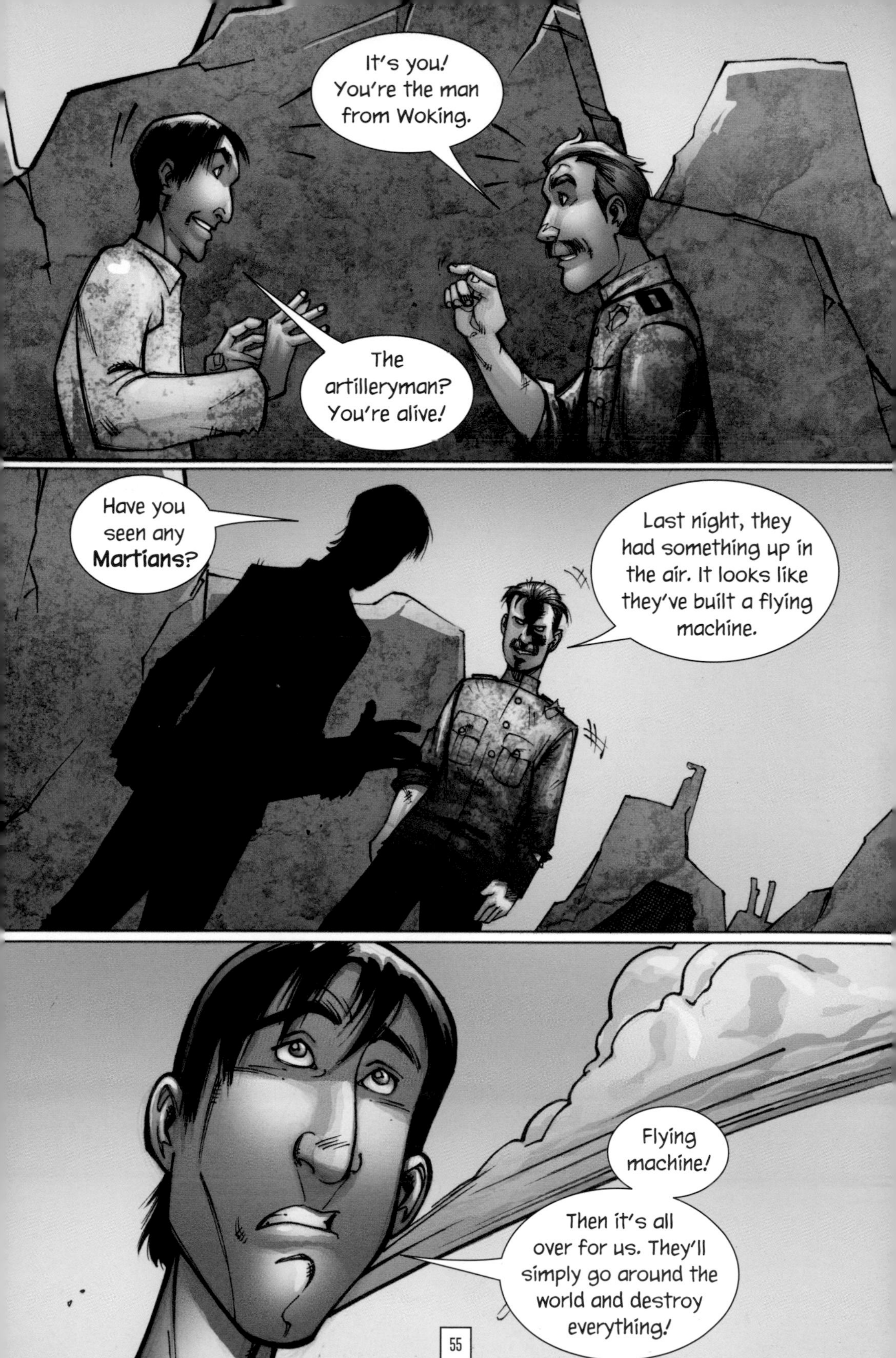
It's you! You're the man from Woking.
The artilleryman? You're alive!
Have you seen any **Martians**?
Last night, they had something up in the air. It looks like they've built a flying machine.
Flying machine!
Then it's all over for us. They'll simply go around the world and destroy everything!

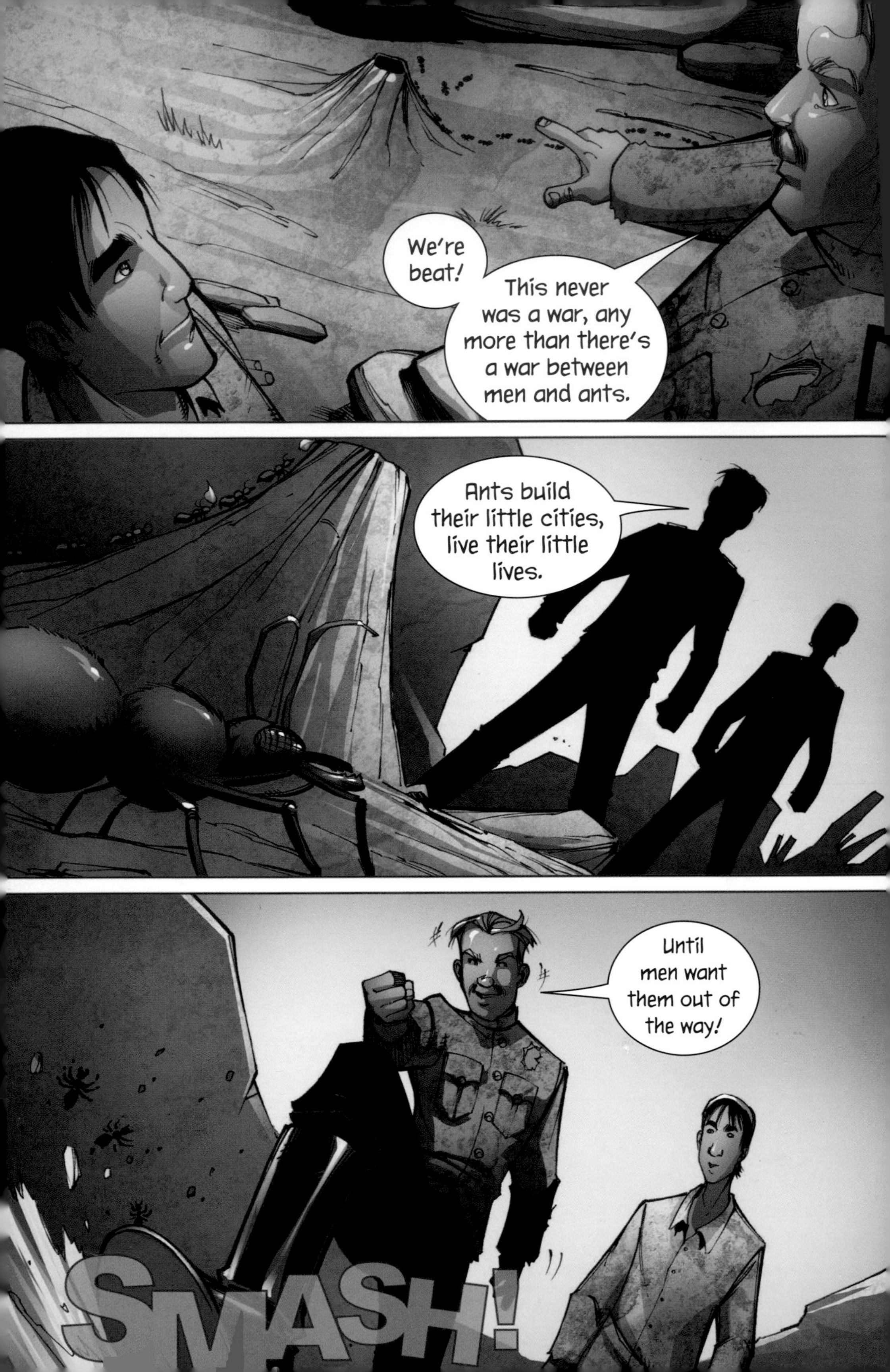
We're beat!
This never was a war, any more than there's a war between men and ants.
Ants build their little cities, live their little lives.
Until men want them out of the way!
SMASH!

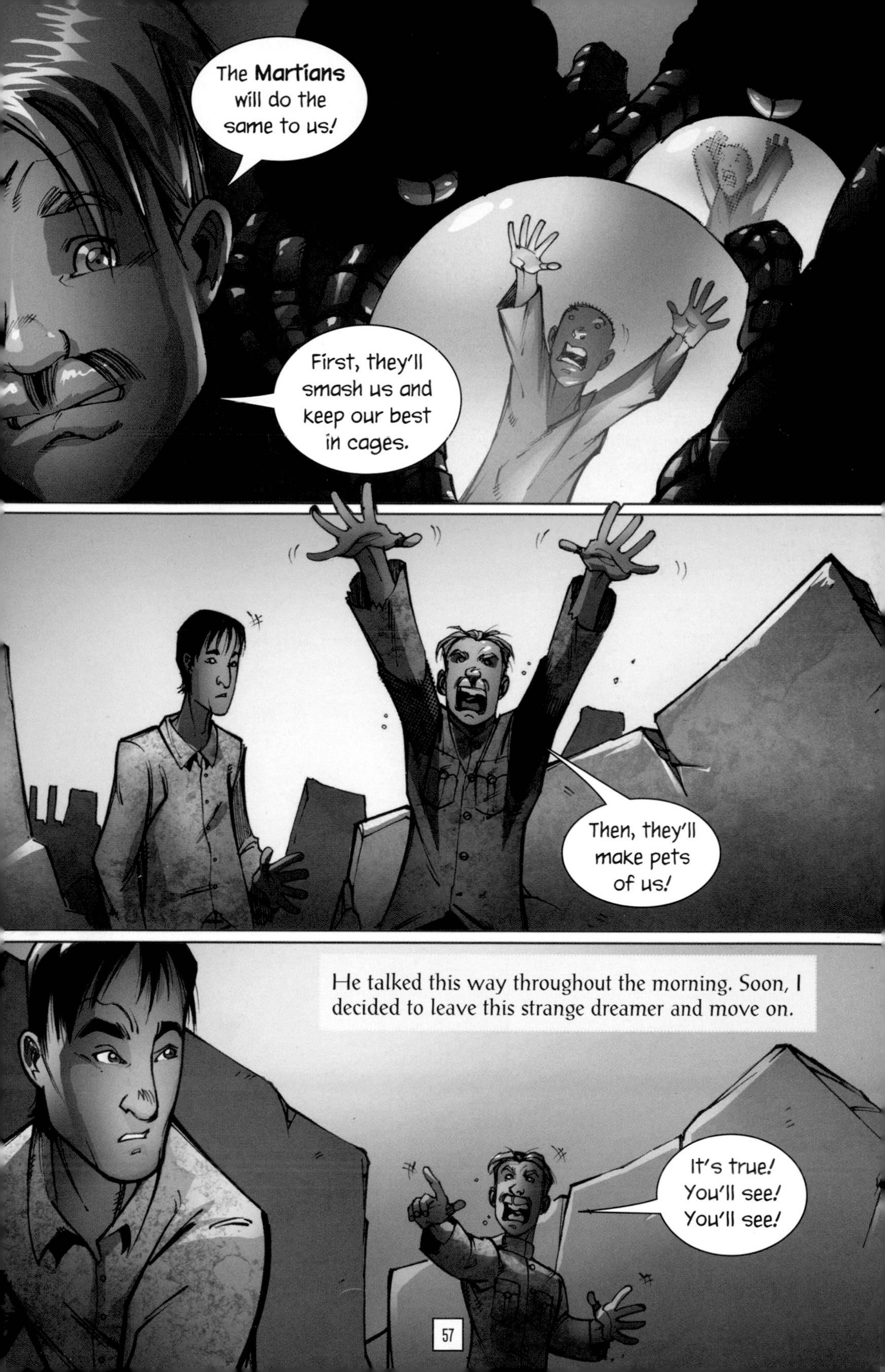

The **Martians** will do the same to us!
First, they'll smash us and keep our best in cages.
Then, they'll make pets of us!
He talked this way throughout the morning. Soon, I decided to leave this strange dreamer and move on.
It's true! You'll see! You'll see!

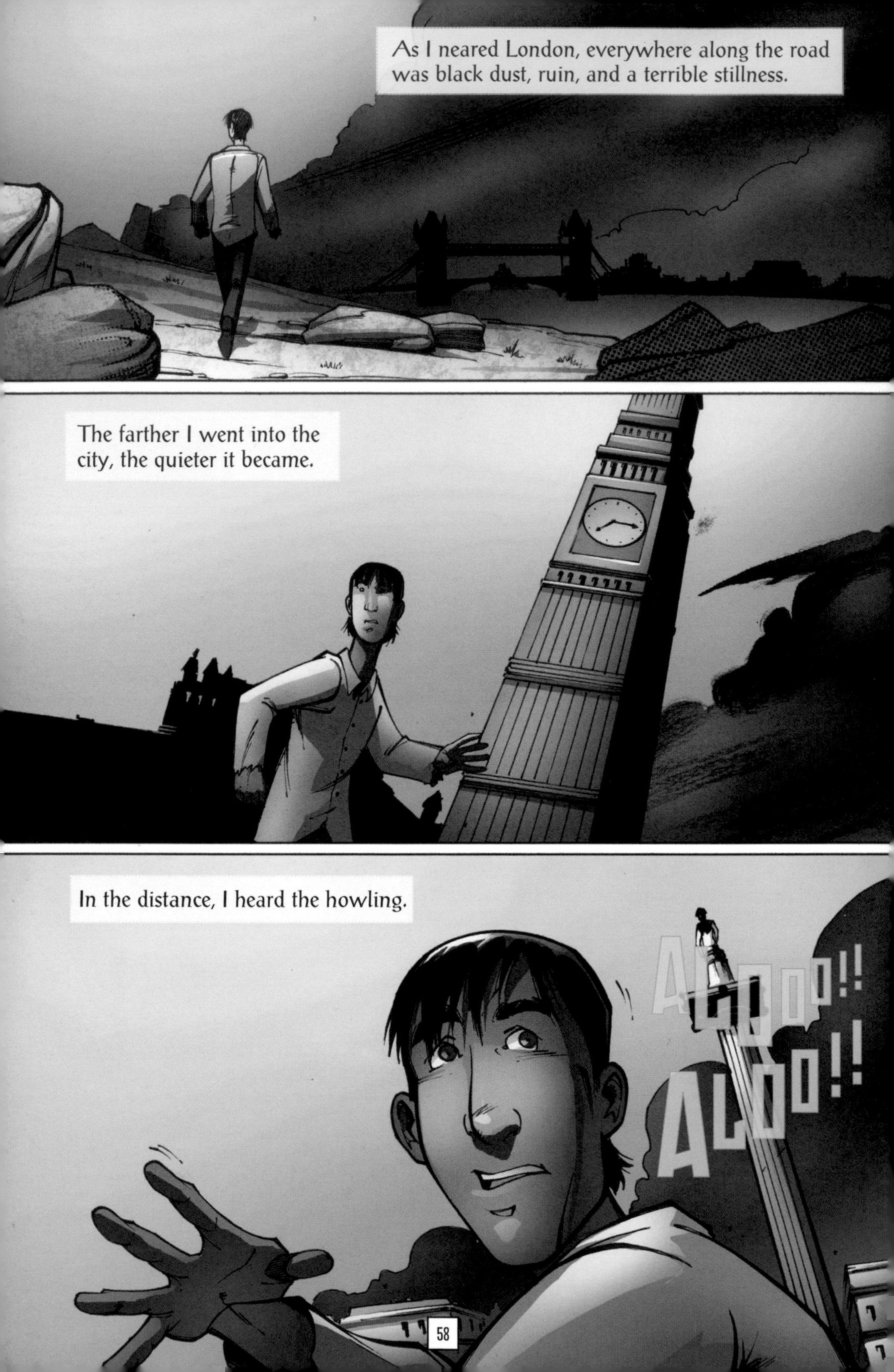
As I neared London, everywhere along the road was black dust, ruin, and a terrible stillness.
The farther I went into the city, the quieter it became.
In the distance, I heard the howling.
ALOOO!!
ALOO!!

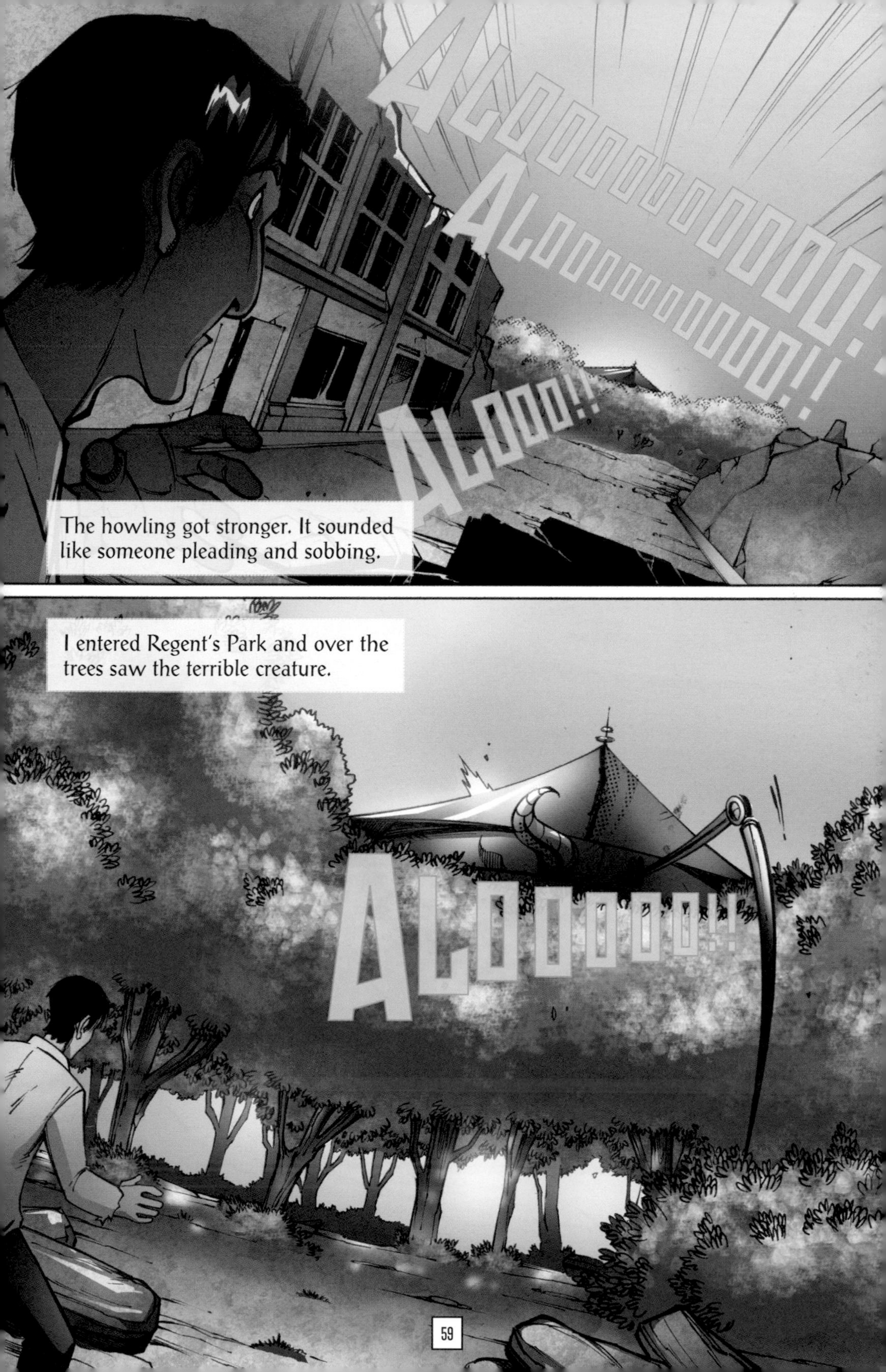
ALOOOOOOOOOOOO!!
ALOOOOOOOOOOO!!
ALOOO!!
The howling got stronger. It sounded like someone pleading and sobbing.
I entered Regent's Park and over the trees saw the terrible creature.
ALOOOOOO!!

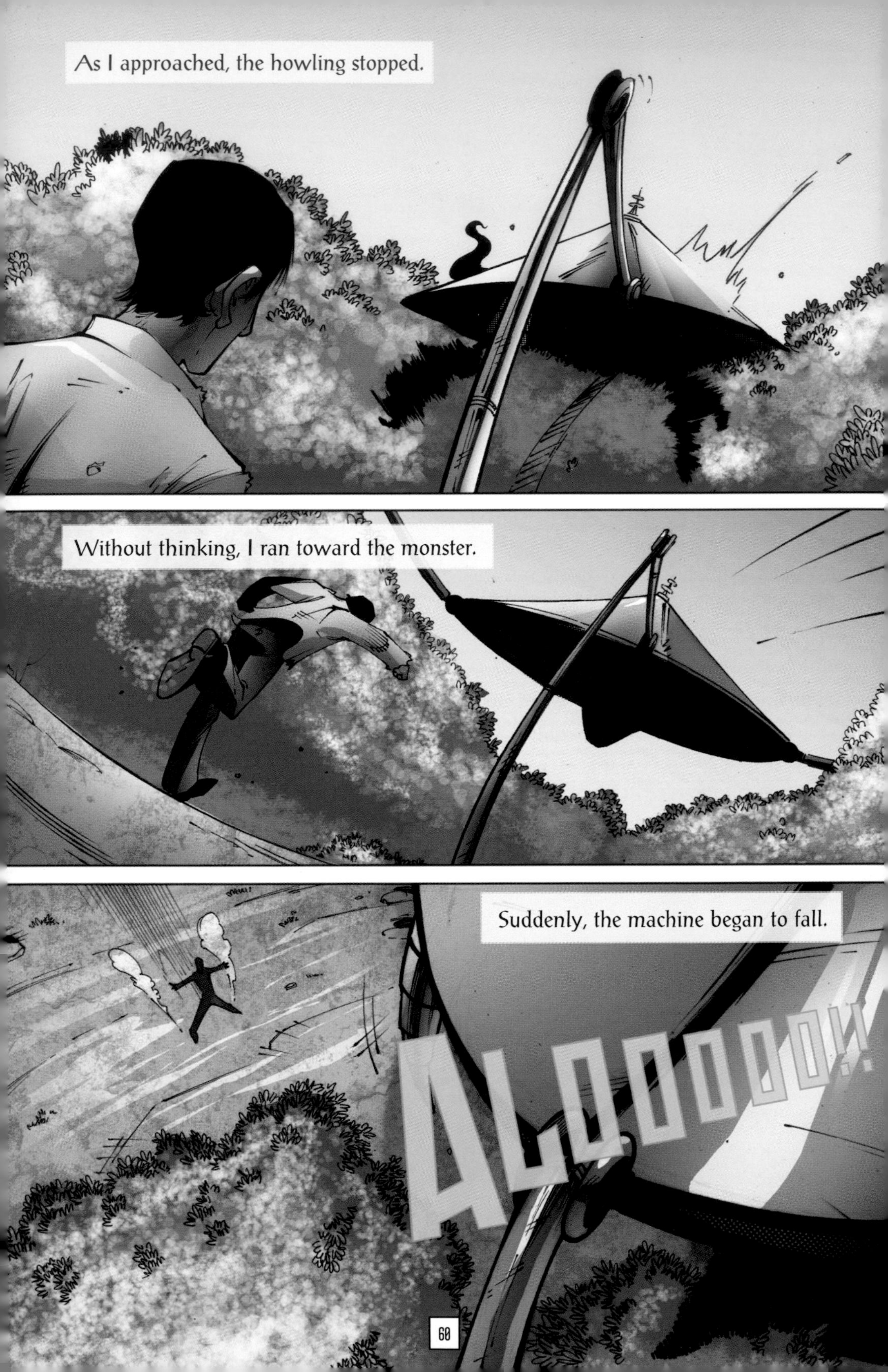
As I approached, the howling stopped.
Without thinking, I ran toward the monster.
Suddenly, the machine began to fall.
ALOOOOO!!

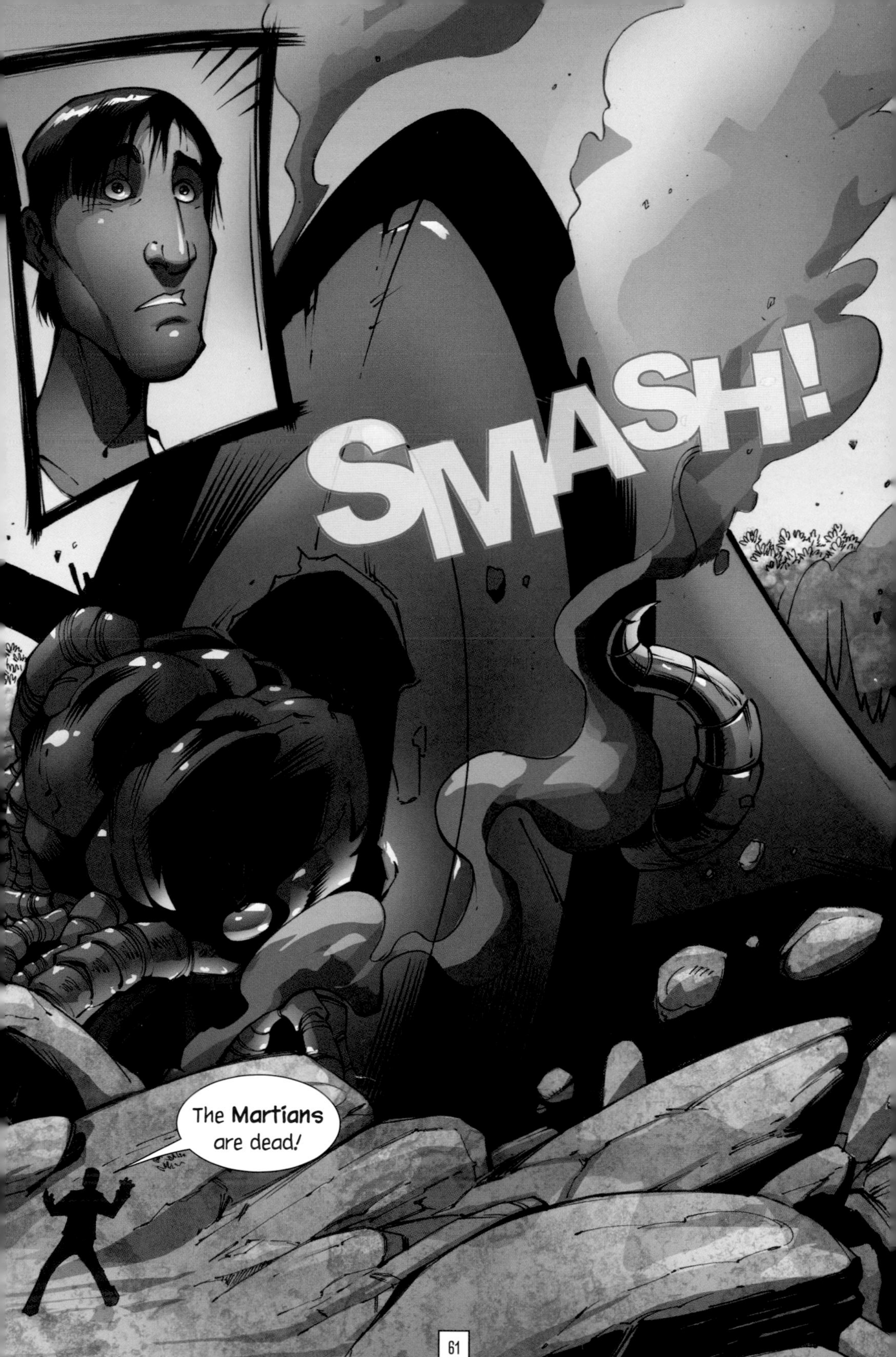
SMASH!
The Martians are dead!

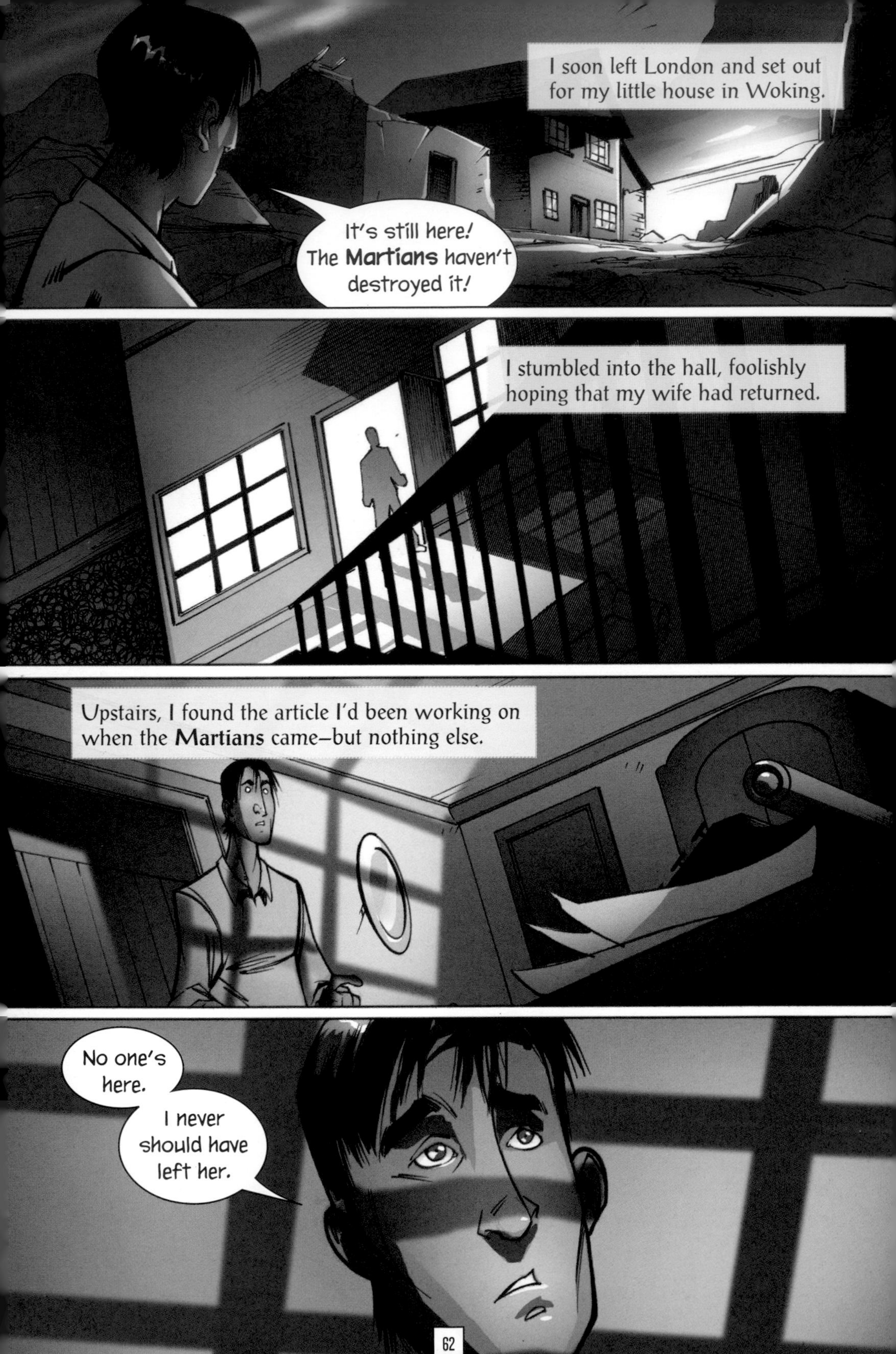

I soon left London and set out for my little house in Woking.
It's still here! The Martians haven't destroyed it!
I stumbled into the hall, foolishly hoping that my wife had returned.
Upstairs, I found the article I'd been working on when the Martians came—but nothing else.
No one's here.
I never should have left her.

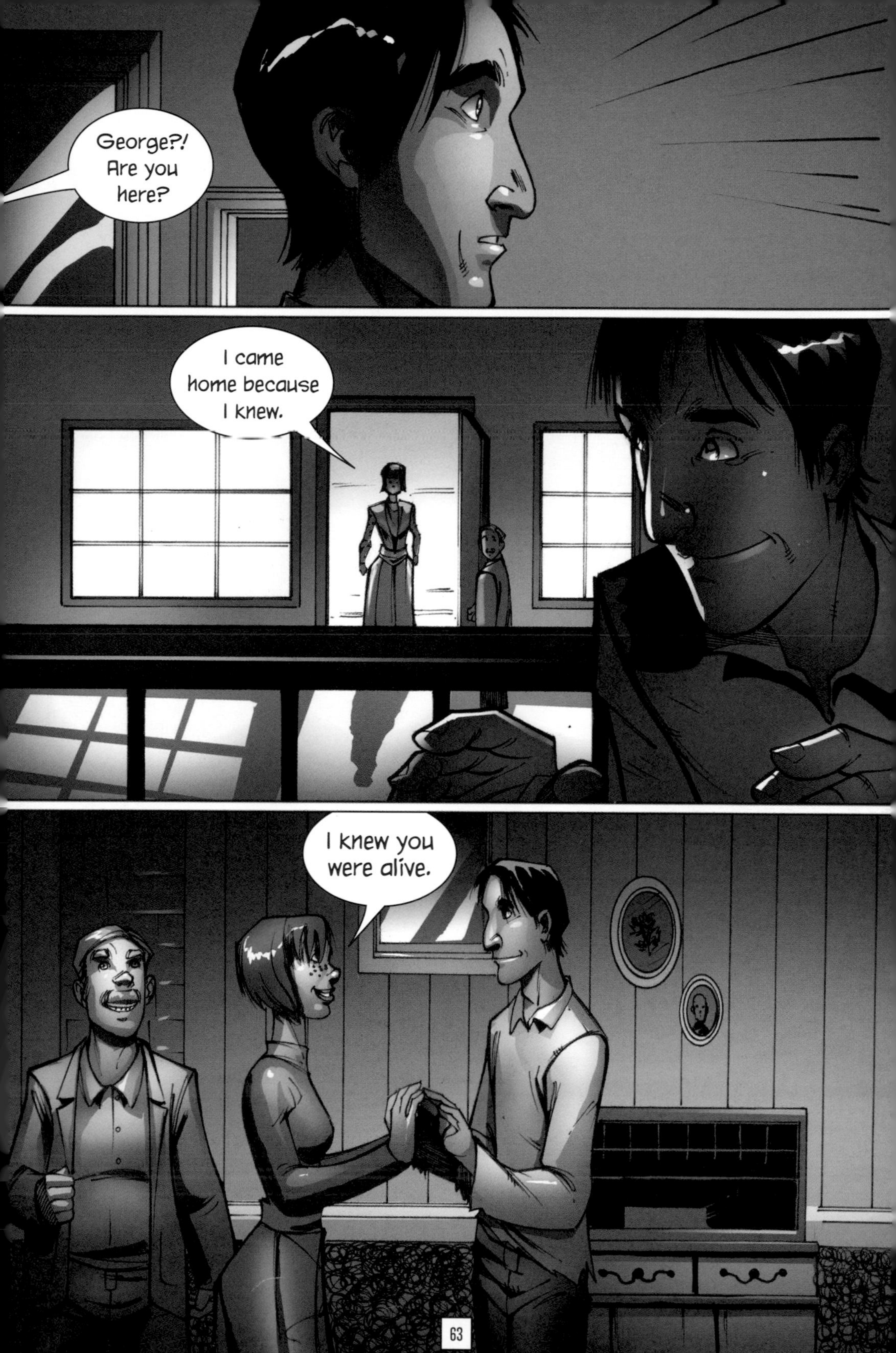
George?! Are you here?
I came home because I knew.
I knew you were alive.

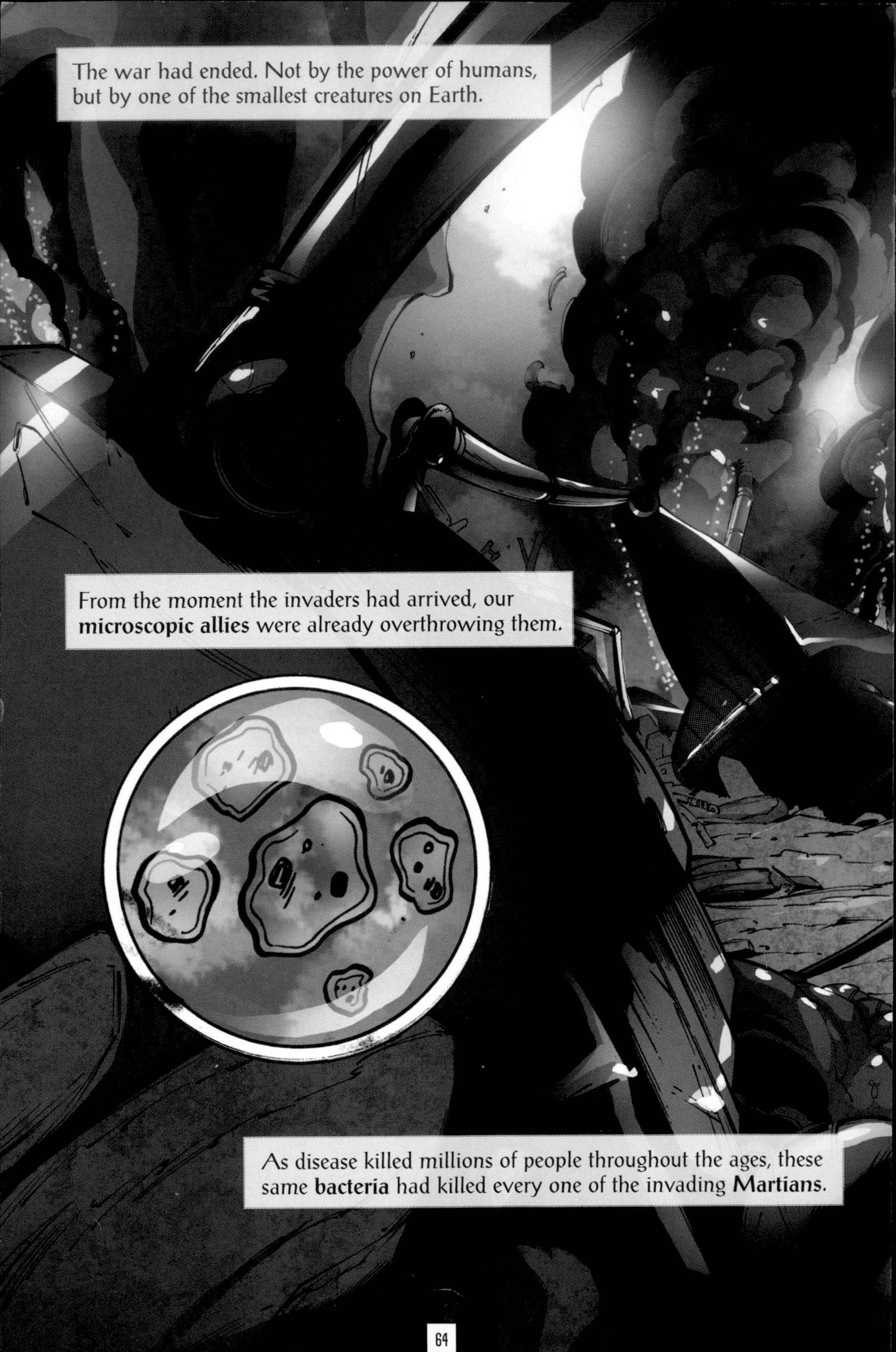
The war had ended. Not by the power of humans, but by one of the smallest creatures on Earth.
From the moment the invaders had arrived, our **microscopic allies** were already overthrowing them.
As disease killed millions of people throughout the ages, these same **bacteria** had killed every one of the invading **Martians**.

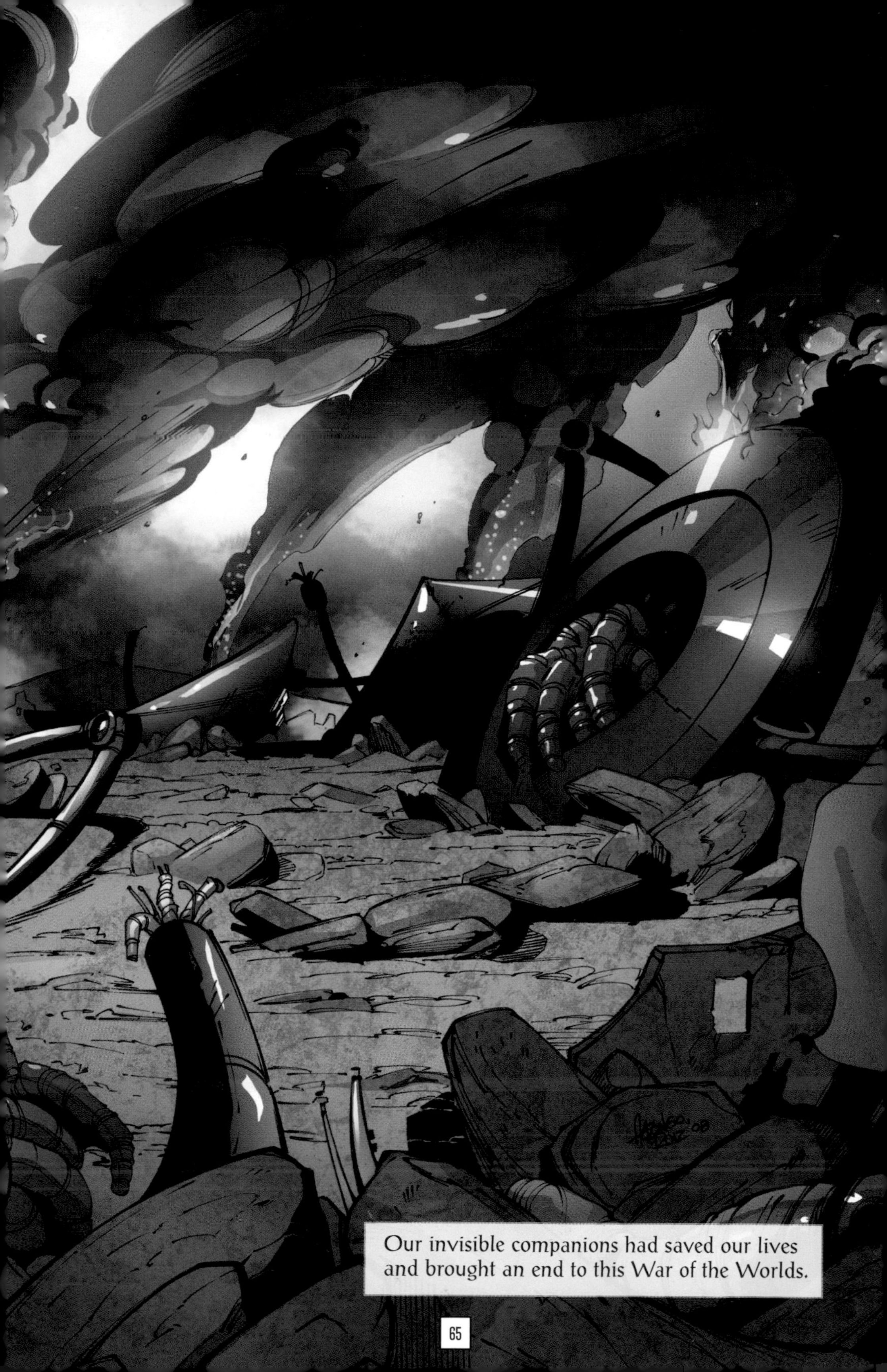
Our invisible companions had saved our lives and brought an end to this War of the Worlds.

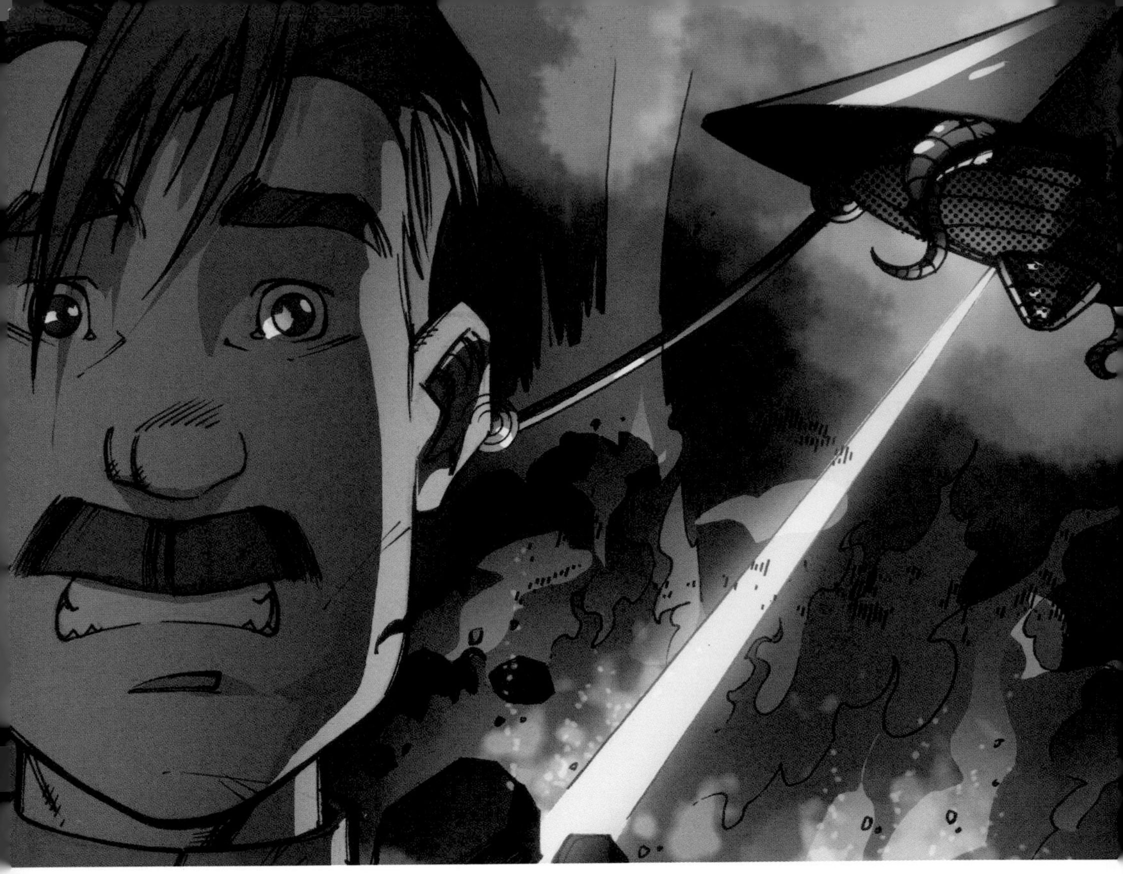

ABOUT THE RETELLING AUTHOR AND ILLUSTRATOR

Davis Worth Miller and **Katherine McLean Brevar** are a married couple who also happen to be full-time writers. Miller has written several best-selling books, including *The Tao of Muhammad Ali*. He has worked on several writing projects with his wife.

José Alfonso Ocampo Ruiz was born in 1975 in Macuspana, Tabasco in Mexico, where the temperature is just as hot as the sauce is. He became a comic book illustrator when he was 17 years old, and has worked on many graphic novels since then. Alfonso has illustrated several graphic novels, including retellings of *Dracula* and *Pinocchio*.

GLOSSARY

abandoned (uh-BAN-duhnd)—empty, or no longer in use

allies (AL-eyes)—people or things that give support and help to another

bacteria (bak-TIHR-ee-uh)—microscopic living things that sometimes cause disease

crater (KRAY-tur)—a large hole in the ground often caused by an explosion

curate (KYOO-rayt)—a person in charge of a church

cylinder (SIL-uhn-dur)—a shape with flat, circular ends and sides shaped like the outside of a tube

Martians (MAR-shuhns)—fictional alien creatures from the planet Mars

meteorite (MEE-tee-ur-rite)—the part of a meteor or space rock that falls to Earth before it has burned up

microscopic (mye-kruh-SKOP-ik)—too small to be seen without a microscope

tentacle (TEN-tuh-kuhl)—one of the long, flexible limbs of some animals, such as an octopus

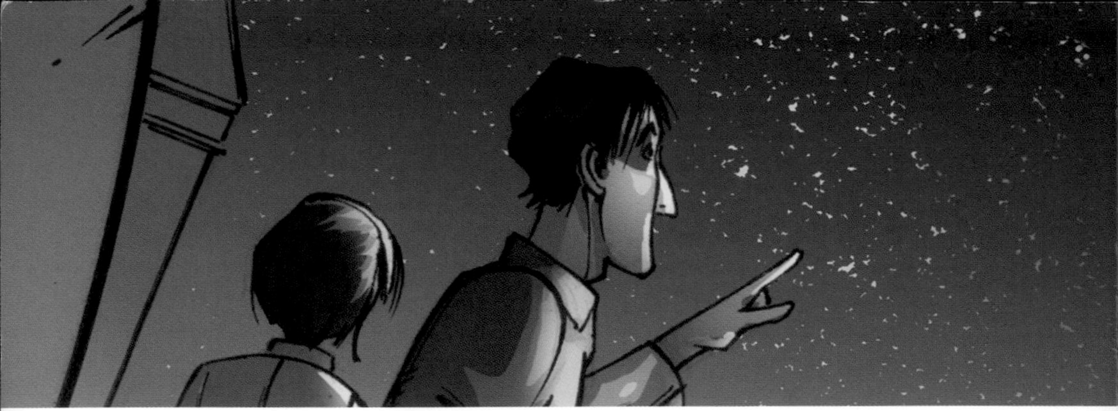

COMMON CORE ALIGNED
READING QUESTIONS

1. **When *The War of the Worlds* was written in 1898, it was widely considered to be a work of science fiction as well as a work of romance. Why do you think that might be?** *("Read and comprehend literature . . . with scaffolding as needed at the high end of the range.")*

2. **The two main characters in the novel are the two brothers. How do their experiences compare and/or contrast?** *("Describe in depth a character, setting, or event in a story.")*

3. **Invasion and war are two significant themes in *The War of the Worlds*. Find specific page numbers, images, and words to support one of these themes.** *("Determine a theme of a story.")*

4. **If you were asked to describe the narrator of the story, what would you say about him? Find specific examples in the text and art to support your answer.** *("Describe in depth a character . . . drawing on specific details in the text.")*

5. **The invasion of Earth by the Martians is the primary plot of the story. Draw a line on a sheet of paper and mark all the significant events that happen as the aliens invade earth (in the order that they occurred).** *("Refer to details and examples in a text when explaining what the text says explicitly and when drawing inferences from the text.")*

COMMON CORE ALIGNED
WRITING QUESTIONS

1. If you were a news reporter who lived during this invasion of Earth by aliens, what would you write in your news report to describe the invasion? What would be important details to share with the people of Earth? *("Draw evidence from literary . . . texts to support analysis.")*

2. Do you feel that *The War of the Worlds* is believable? What evidence from the text makes you feel something like this could or couldn't happen? *("Write opinion pieces on topics or texts, supporting a point of view with reasons and information.")*

3. What is your favorite part of the story, and why? *("Write informative/ explanatory texts to examine a topic and convey ideas.")*

4. If you were one of the Martians, why might you be invading Earth? Write and develop a one-page explanation for why you and the other Martians invaded another planet. *("Write narratives to develop real or imagined experiences or events.")*

5. *The War of the Worlds* is the first significant literary text about the invasion of Earth by aliens. Can you think of any movies, television shows, books, or video games that are about aliens? Write a list of examples. Next to each one, cite a similar example from text of this book. *("Draw evidence from literary . . . texts to support analysis.")*

READ THEM ALL!

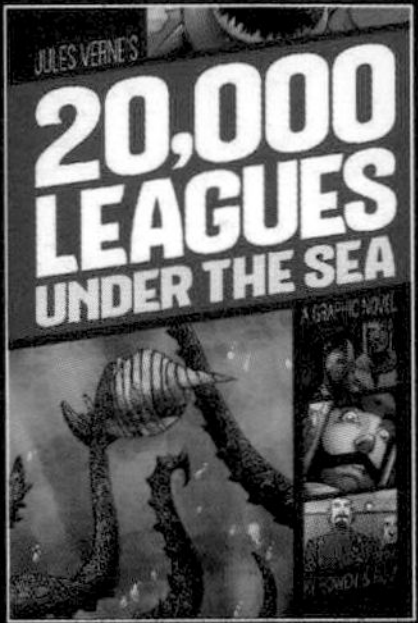
JULES VERNE'S
20,000 LEAGUES UNDER THE SEA
A GRAPHIC NOVEL

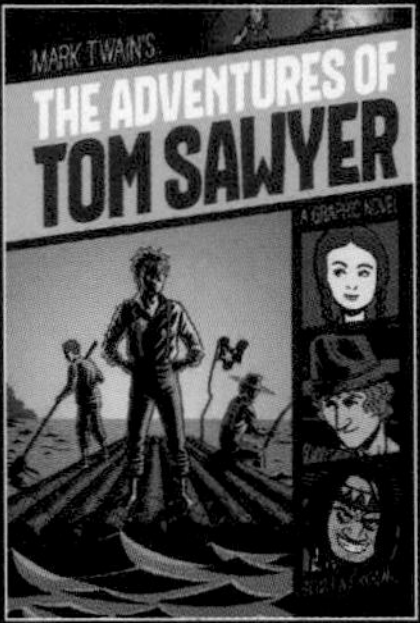
MARK TWAIN'S
THE ADVENTURES OF TOM SAWYER
A GRAPHIC NOVEL

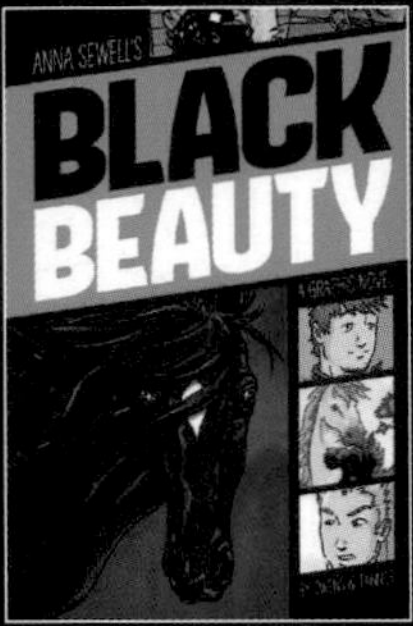
ANNA SEWELL'S
BLACK BEAUTY
A GRAPHIC NOVEL

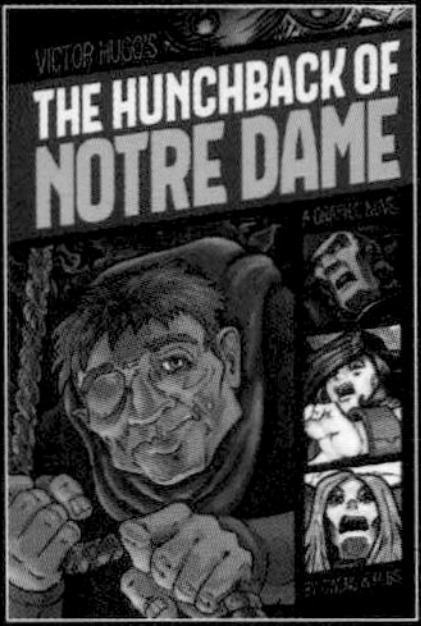
VICTOR HUGO'S
THE HUNCHBACK OF NOTRE DAME
A GRAPHIC NOVEL

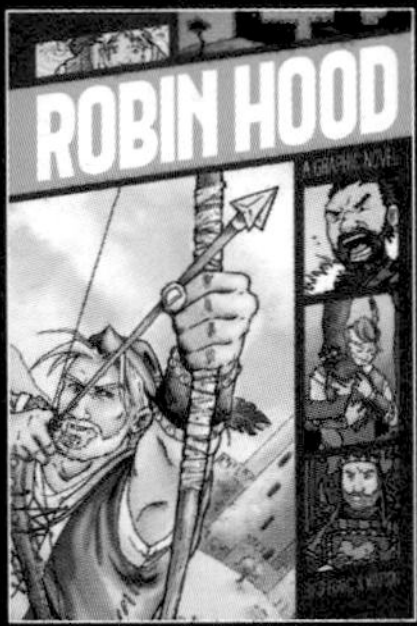
ROBIN HOOD
A GRAPHIC NOVEL

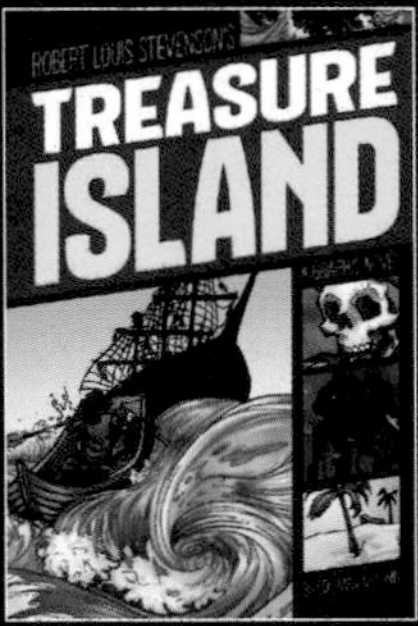
ROBERT LOUIS STEVENSON'S
TREASURE ISLAND

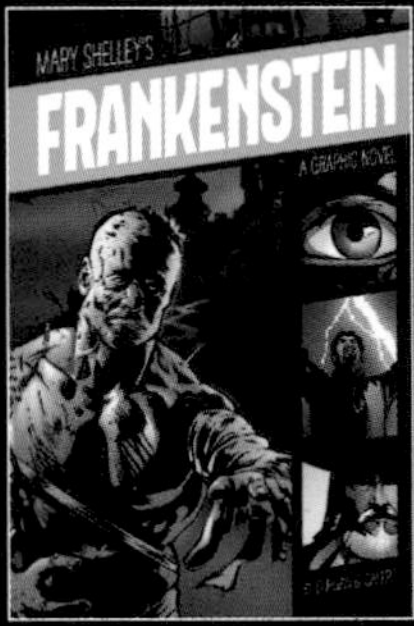
MARY SHELLEY'S
FRANKENSTEIN
A GRAPHIC NOVEL

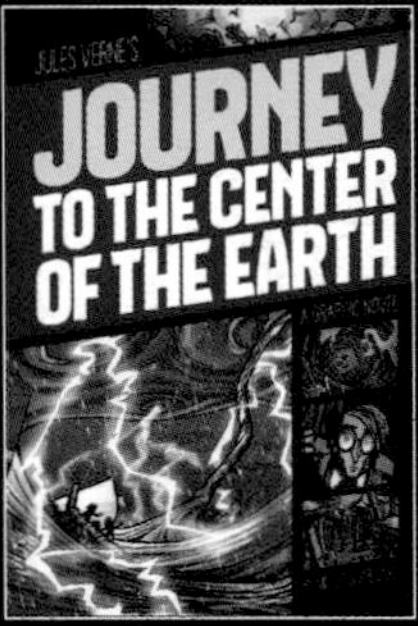
JULES VERNE'S
JOURNEY TO THE CENTER OF THE EARTH

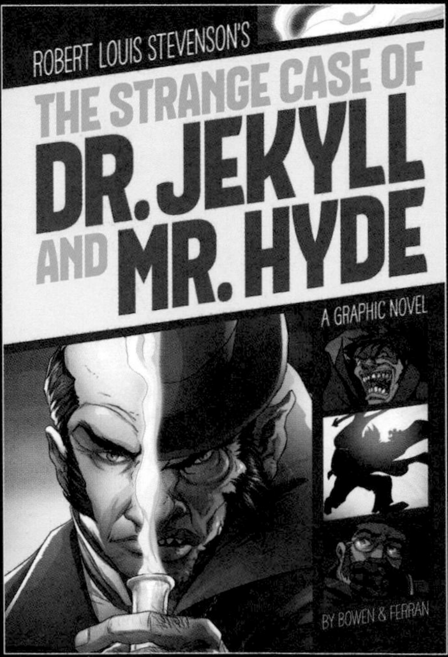
ROBERT LOUIS STEVENSON'S
THE STRANGE CASE OF DR. JEKYLL AND MR. HYDE
A GRAPHIC NOVEL
BY BOWEN & FERRAN

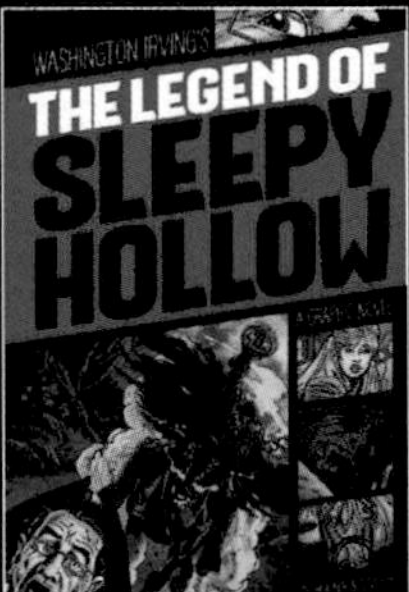
WASHINGTON IRVING'S
THE LEGEND OF SLEEPY HOLLOW

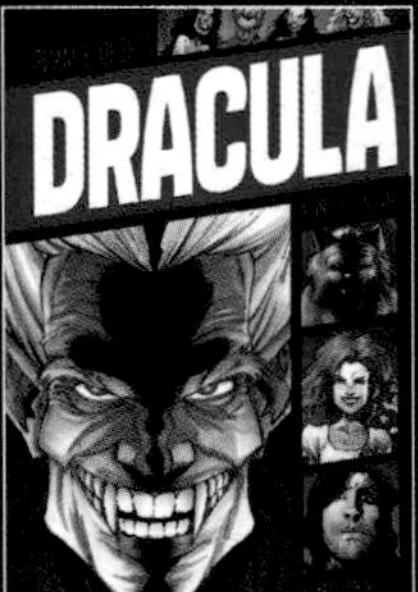
DRACULA

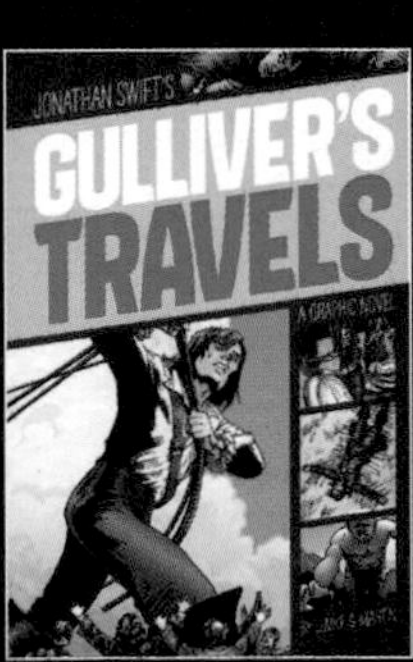
JONATHAN SWIFT'S
GULLIVER'S TRAVELS
A GRAPHIC NOVEL

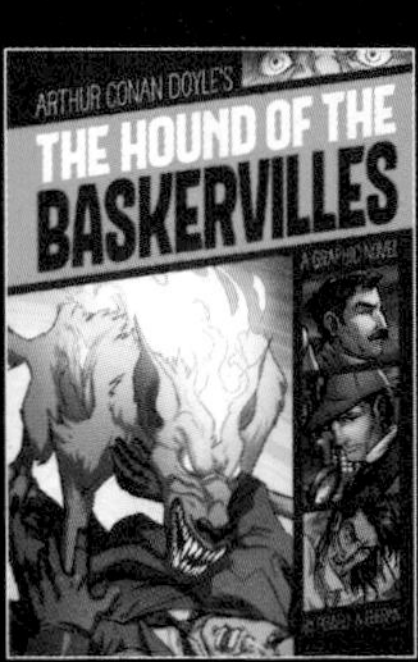
ARTHUR CONAN DOYLE'S
THE HOUND OF THE BASKERVILLES
A GRAPHIC NOVEL

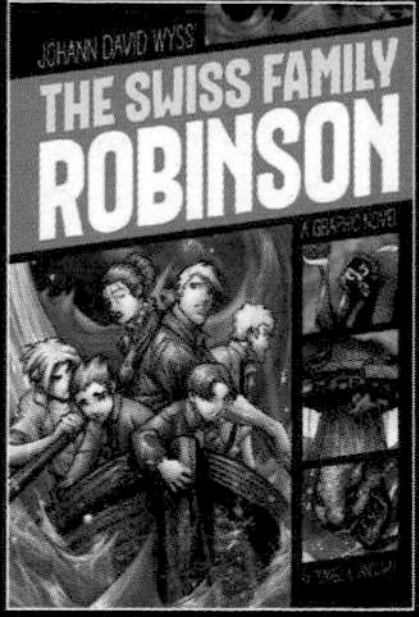
JOHANN DAVID WYSS'
THE SWISS FAMILY ROBINSON
A GRAPHIC NOVEL

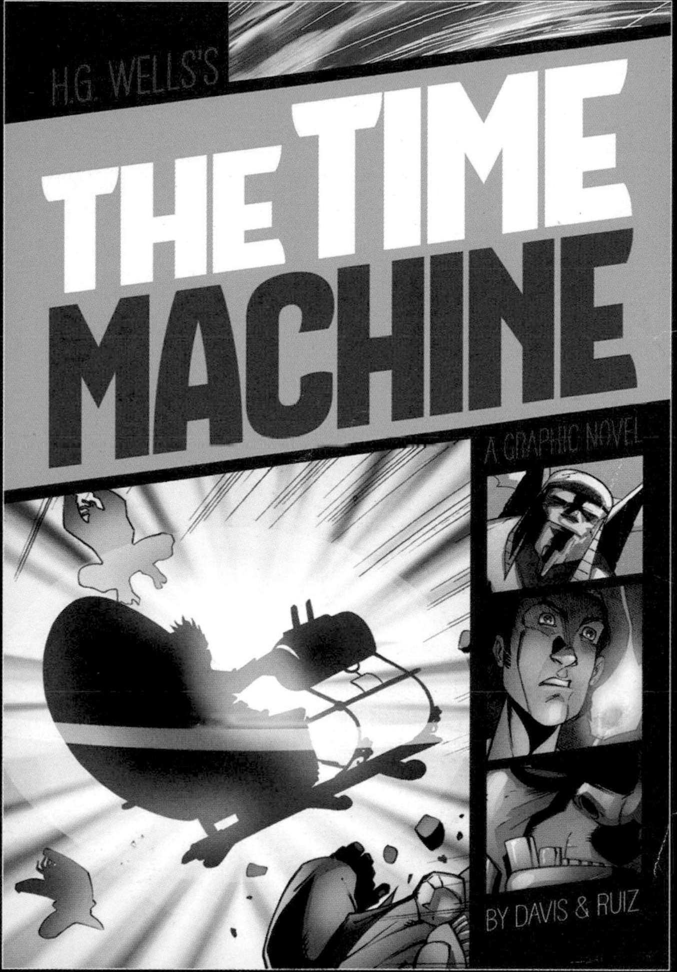
H.G. WELLS'S
THE TIME MACHINE
A GRAPHIC NOVEL
BY DAVIS & RUIZ

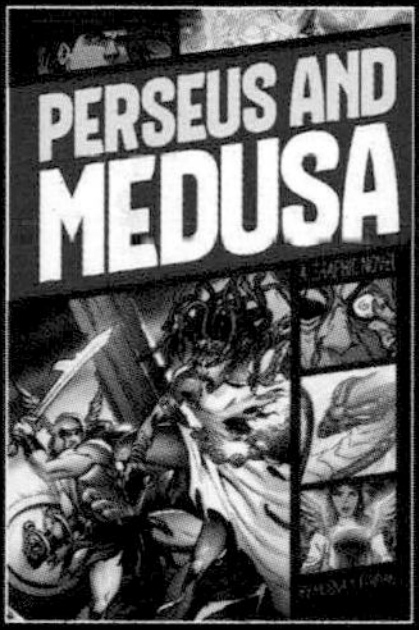
PERSEUS AND MEDUSA
A GRAPHIC NOVEL

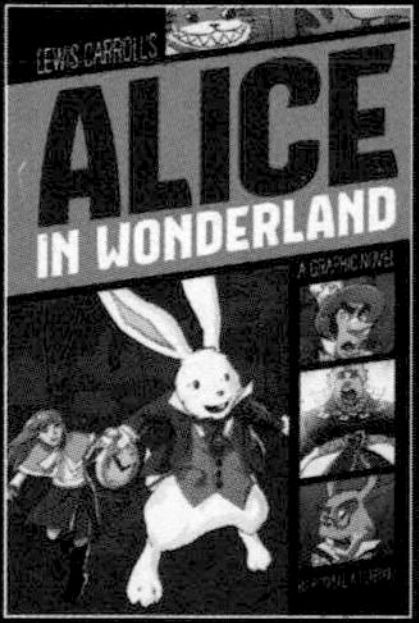
LEWIS CARROLL'S
ALICE IN WONDERLAND
A GRAPHIC NOVEL

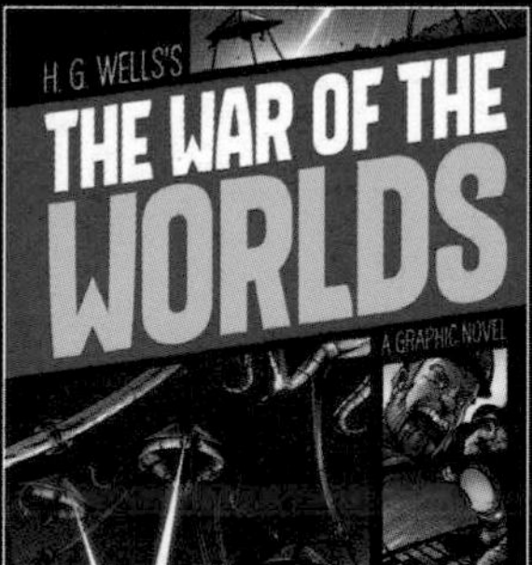
H. G. WELLS'S
THE WAR OF THE WORLDS
A GRAPHIC NOVEL

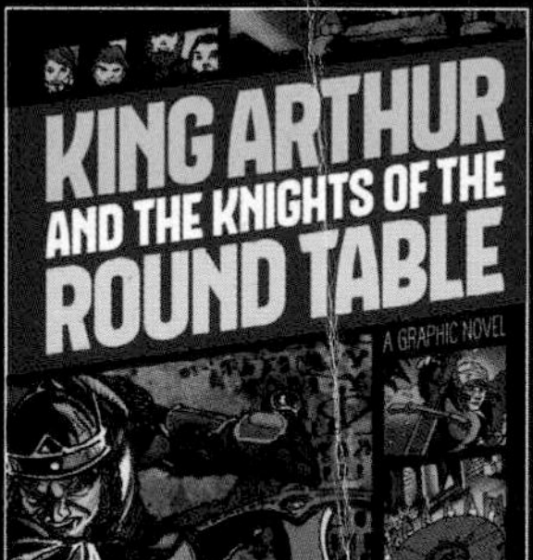
KING ARTHUR AND THE KNIGHTS OF THE ROUND TABLE
A GRAPHIC NOVEL

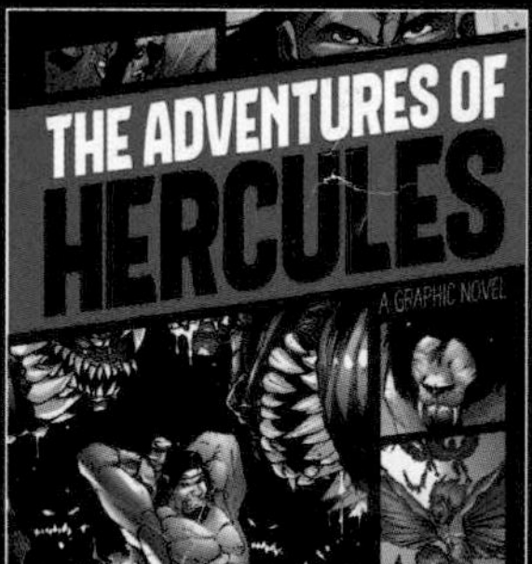
THE ADVENTURES OF HERCULES
A GRAPHIC NOVEL

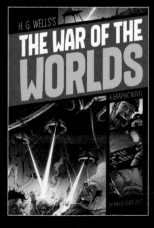

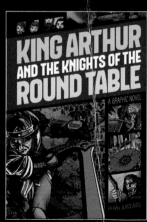

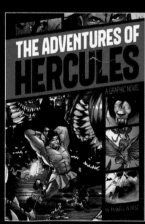